$10.00

1/4

Fab Life Series

Time to Shine

Also by Nikki Carter

STEP TO THIS

IT IS WHAT IT IS

IT'S ALL GOOD

COOL LIKE THAT

NOT A GOOD LOOK

ALL THE WRONG MOVES

DOING MY OWN THING

ON THE FLIP SIDE

Published by Kensington Publishing Corporation

Time to Shine

A Fab Life Novel

NIKKI CARTER

Dafina KTeen Books
KENSINGTON PUBLISHING CORP.
http://www.kensingtonbooks.com

DAFINA KTEEN BOOKS are published by

Kensington Publishing Corp.
119 West 40th Street
New York, NY 10018

All Kensington titles, imprints, and distributed lines are available at special quantity discounts for bulk purchases for sales promotion, premiums, fund-raising, educational, or institutional use.

Special book excerpts or customized printings can also be created to fit specific needs. For details, write or phone the office of the Kensington Special Sales Manager: Attn.: Special Sales Department. Kensington Publishing Corp., 119 West 40th Street, New York, NY 10018. Phone: 1-800-221-2647.

K logo Reg. US Pat. & TM Off.
Sunburst logo Reg. US Pat. & TM Off.

ISBN-13: 978-0-7582-7270-6
ISBN-10: 0-7582-7270-7

First Printing: November 2012

10 9 8 7 6 5 4 3 2

Printed in the United States of America

Acknowledgments

Hey everybody! I hope y'all enjoy Sunday's new adventure, 'cause I sure had a blast writing it. I want to thank everyone who helped make it possible! God, my hubby, Brent (Crock-Pot chef—yeah!), my babies (Briana, Brittany, Brynn, Brent II, Brooke), and the entire team at Kensington Books (especially Mercedes)!

I'm blessed to have some ride-or-die friends like Sunday has, so I have to shout them out! Shawana, Lil' Robin, Lee-Lee, Tippy T, Dee, and Rhonda—love y'all to a million little pieces!

I want to thank my Twitter crew, Boss Tionna Smalls, Brittany Howard, Nikki Turner, Jaelyn, and Jasmine's World. Thanks for the retweets, ladies!

To all of my readers, and to every teacher and librarian who recommends my books: Thank you!

Enjoy. . . .

1

"**S**unday Tolliver! Are you on your way to Mystique and Zillionaire's wedding?"

The paparazzo catches me off guard by jumping from behind a building as I exit my parked car in front of Mt. Pleasant Baptist Church in downtown Atlanta. Really? This bird is hiding at four o'clock in the morning trying to get the scoop? I mean who is checking for Mystique wedding details at four in the morning? And anyway this is not the location for Mystique's wedding. It's actually one of the decoy spots. I will be picked up by another car to take me to the final location.

"I'm on my way into this church," I say.

The annoyed almost-reporter cocks her head to one side and sucks her teeth. She looks like she doesn't know whether or not to believe me. I certainly don't look like I'm going to a wedding. I'm wearing sweatpants, and my hair is in a loose bun on the top of my head. But there's a full wardrobe and makeup crew at the real venue, so I don't have to worry about looking glam right now.

"You're one of her bridesmaids, aren't you?" the reporter girl asks.

I lean in closely and whisper, "I'll never tell."

The frustrated reporter rolls her eyes again and storms off, perhaps looking for someone more willing to spill their guts about the so-called wedding of the year.

I won't share the details because, as a pop star myself, I don't like my business in the streets (or on the Internet) either.

I stride away from the irritated blogger chick. She can be camped out here for the next few hours and she won't be any closer to the truth than she is now. The plan is for members of the wedding party to be picked up by shuttle bus at four-thirty in the morning. Then we will be taken to the top-secret wedding location. The wedding party doesn't even know where it is.

I can't believe Mystique was able to pull off something this complex when she and Zac (Zillionaire) only decided to get married a few weeks ago. News of Zac's love child hit the blogs and the next thing you know those two are going to the chapel, getting married.

When she asked me to be her maid of honor, I was kind of shocked. It's not like we're really close or anything like that. She gave me my first record deal and basically introduced me to the world as her protégée, but something happened in these past few months. All of a sudden she got competitive, and did a couple of things that could be construed as hateration.

I duck into the church and hand my car keys to a security guy standing at the door. He will be in charge of driving my car from the church to another parking area—not where the wedding will be held—but another fake location to throw off the paparazzi. Yeah, it's super cloak and dagger up in this piece.

Then I see him.

The new ex-boyfriend of mine. Sam.

Ugh.

Like, can I ask a side bar question? Why do boys have to lie all the time? Sam told me that he didn't hook up with Rielle on prom night, and that was a big, fat, gigantic lie. He says he only lied because he didn't think I'd be his girlfriend if I knew, and he's probably right. I would've soooo kept it moving. But now, I really like (almost kind of love) Sam and he's hurt me.

Maybe I would've believed that he was all done with Rielle after prom, but apparently he's still dealing with her. He even bought her a laptop! Do I care that he did it because she's poor and her grandmother heard that he got a million-plus-dollar check? Um, no. We do not do good deeds for side pieces.

And why is he smiling at me? Ugh. I can't stand him.

He's Zac's best man, for some ridiculous reason. They aren't even friends. At all. Sam is his employee. Zac and Mystique are probably trying to orchestrate a reunion or some stupidity like that. But I don't care. Not trying to hear that.

Sam crosses the church sanctuary to where I'm standing in the back. He's still smiling like an idiot. I roll my eyes.

"So, they're sending a car for us," he says. "It should be here soon."

I give him a tight nod and start playing with my iPhone. I make a huge production out of putting my earbuds in, so he can tell that I'm listening to my music.

I wish my girls Gia, Piper, and Meagan were here with me. They didn't rank high enough on the celebrity list to get an invite to Mystique's wedding. They're not celebrities at all—they're my friends from Spelman. Gia is my roommate.

Mystique told me that I could invite one of them as my guest since I don't have a date, but I decided against it. The two I didn't invite would inevitably be mad at me, and I'm anti-drama right now.

So, I invited DeShawn. He's a hottie who goes to Georgia State and plays on the football team with Gia's boyfriend, Ricky. DeShawn also models and was in one of my music videos. He's cool, he's a friend, and he flirts with me. It doesn't matter that I'm not in the boyfriend type mood. Having DeShawn with me at the wedding will, at least, keep Sam out of my face. I hope.

The wedding guests have to park their cars at a different location, and then they'll be driven to the top-secret wedding location by another shuttle bus. Mystique has sold exclusive rights to her wedding photos to *People* magazine, so it's, like, imperative that nobody take any pictures—paparazzi or guests. They're even hijacking people's cell phones at the door.

It's that serious.

After a few minutes, I hear another car pull up outside the church. Sam and I are given dark jackets and baseball caps to put on, as we exit the back of the building. We look like some ghetto spies.

Once we're in the car, I notice that the driver is one of Zac's security guys. He drives us through Atlanta to a beautiful castle on Peachtree, called Rhodes Hall.

"I can't believe they're getting married here. Right in the middle of everything!" I exclaim to no one in particular.

Sam replies, "This is the perfect location. No one would even suspect that they were getting married this close to downtown Atlanta."

I narrow my eyes in Sam's direction. I was not talking to him. Okay . . . so I know there are only two other people in the car besides me, and since I don't know the driver, it's pretty logical for Sam to assume that I'm talking to him.

But, since he also knows that I can't stand his guts right now, he shouldn't assume anything.

We're dropped off at the back gate of the castle, but since it's still dark outside no one can see us. Amazingly, there are no paparazzi hiding here. Maybe, it's because we took a roundabout way to get here. The church where we got picked up from is like ten minutes from the actual venue, but it took us forty minutes to get here.

When Sam and I walk into the building . . . wait. I do not like "Sam and I" put together in one sentence. That is so . . . *ugh!*

When I walk into the building (we don't care what Sam is doing) I see Mystique barking out orders like the Bridezilla from the pits of Hades.

"Mother, please tell me that my veil is here. The custom-made diamond-encrusted veil that cost three million dollars to produce is here, right? Because if it's not here, someone's head is gonna roll."

Ms. Layla, Mystique's mom, puts a hand on her daughter's back. It's a calming move, but it doesn't seem like it works.

"Honey, the veil is here. I just unpacked it. It is with Zac's security team now. Try to stay calm. You don't want to look frazzled in your wedding photos."

"Okay, mother . . . I'm trying. I'm really trying. Where's Sunday? Is she here yet?"

"Present and accounted for," I say from the back of the room.

Mystique flies back to greet me and embraces me with a bear hug. Who is this? I'm afraid I have not met this emotional and affectionate person masquerading as Mystique.

"Sunday, I'm so glad you're here. I can't have anything else going wrong."

"I'm here too," Sam says.

Mystique smiles at Sam and then says to me, "Sunday . . . can you please, please be nice to Sam today? I want you smiling in my pictures."

I reply through clenched teeth. "I'll try."

Mystique seems to accept my reply. I'm glad because it's the best I can do. She rushes off to fuss at the florist, who apparently has brought an incorrect flower.

"Does this look like a calla lily?" Mystique asks in a high pitched roar.

I take a seat and wait for someone to tell me what to do. I don't want to get in Mystique's path. Not today.

I know that if I ever get married (and that is so not in the plans any time soon), I don't want it to be like this.

2

By the time the wedding begins, this castle is jam-packed with everyone who's anyone in the music industry. From my post on the upstairs balcony landing, I can see people as they arrive. I can barely move since I'm poured into this form fitting rose colored gown. It's a good thing I didn't eat that pizza last night, because my stomach bulge would definitely show! I can also still hear Mystique's insane barking of orders, but I got into hair, makeup, and my dress over an hour ago, just so I could stay out of her way.

I watch as the entire Reign Records crew shows up in a Hummer limo. Leave it to Evan Wilborn to make a spectacle of himself on someone else's big day. He steps out of the car and helps my cousin, Dreya, out of the car. They are both wearing white, from head to toe. Dreya's dress is floor length, fitted, and covered in something sparkly. She's also got on jewel-encrusted shoes. She's traded in her usual spiky hairdo, for a long flowing wig that's pinned up on one side.

She looks nothing like Drama the R & B-slash-rap star. She looks like a Hollywood starlet on her way to a red carpet event. It is a good look for her.

Other Reign Records artists, Bethany and Dilly, also emerge from the limo, also wearing white. Big D, my manager and one of the head honchos of Reign Records and his girlfriend, Shelly, get out on the other side of the car, and they all have on white. Big D has really outdone himself with a white top hat and cane, with his plus-sized white suit, and Shelly's barely there dress stops right underneath her bottom. She covers the rest of her legs with fishnet stockings and thigh-high leather boots. All three of the ladies are wearing fur, since it is wintertime, and cold as all get out in Atlanta.

They all look out of pocket with this white on, like it's a summer wedding. Reign Records is tripping right now. Isn't there a rule about wearing white after Labor Day? I don't think it's allowed. And everybody knows that you don't wear white to someone's wedding. I don't think anyone told Evan or anyone else from Reign Records.

The flashiest accessory to their entire ensembles is the Reign Records medallion that everyone wears around their necks. My hand absentmindedly touches my neck, where my medallion would be if I was wearing it. For some reason, I can't bring myself to buy into the whole "family" thing that Evan has envisioned for his record label. We might all be label mates, but the bottom line is we're all competition. Dreya isn't fooling me one bit with this unity act, especially when it comes to Bethany, who she pretty much hates for hooking up with her ex-boyfriend.

The only people in the limo not wearing all white are my mom, Shawn, and my aunt Charlie, Dreya's mom. My mother is wearing a very elegant, long-sleeved, navy-blue gown that I bought her, with shoes to match. Aunt Charlie has on a skin-tight red suit with red stockings and gold shoes. I shake my head at the sight of her. Who wears red to a wedding? But nobody can check Aunt Charlie's style without hearing a mouthful of holleration. Since I don't feel like hearing her mouth, I will keep mum on the subject of her outfit.

I smile when I see DeShawn get dropped off by the valet at the front door of the castle. He was surprised when I asked him to be my date for the wedding, and of course he said yes. Number one, he's been trying to get with me for a minute, and two, he's a model, always looking to network and land a gig. Along with his football scholarship at Georgia State, he models to pay his bills. I am not mad at him for that.

I asked DeShawn to be my date, so that in no uncertain terms can Sam understand that I am no longer his girlfriend. Sam started out being someone I totally vibed with on every level. Our music was perfect, he *got* me and I got him too. We had a little drama in the very beginning, when another rapper, this guy named Truth, was trying to push up on me too. I thought that once we made it past all that, we would be together forever.

Then, I found out a whole string of lies that he told me, starting with him getting high on drugs at a party and hooking up with a groupie. But that wasn't even the worst thing! When I learned that he was basically caking this girl named Rielle, buying her computers and who knows what else, I was done. Sam's lies are beyond the level of acceptable, so he's been kicked to the curb.

I can't say that it doesn't hurt me. It hurts like crazy. He's the first guy I ever let myself fall all the way for, and I'm the type of chick who doesn't fall easily. I let him in, with his music and his witticism, and he paid me back with a bunch of lies. So, now I have a new mantra. Love is for suckas.

I'm about to get mine, money and career wise, and let all romance come second, if at all. Matter of fact, I don't even need romance. Who needs boys when they don't do anything but tell lies? Even DeShawn, as cool and as fine as he is, is suspect as well.

It sucks that the rest of my friends can't be here to offer their support. My crazy roommate Gia would know exactly what to say to make me laugh in spite of how insane this all feels. Piper and Meagan would be a distraction with all their bickering about the sorority they plan to join and the husbands they plan to land before they graduate from school. But of course, they were not invited to Mystique's wedding, because they're not industry people. My world is divided between the music industry and my college crew. Sometimes the two groups mix, and sometimes, like today, they do not.

Music starts in the main room of the castle, a signal to everyone that this show is about to be on the road. Ms. Layla steps out onto the landing, looking regal in her silver two-piece gown with a knee-high split. She is fly for an older woman. She winks over at me as she holds the arms of her escorts, two of Zac the Zillionaire's artists.

I wink back at her and smile. People can say what they want about Ms. Layla, but she's always got Mystique's back like one thousand percent. She reminds me of how my mother holds it down for me.

As soon as Ms. Layla heard about Zac's love child, she sprang into action and started orchestrating a fix to the messy situation. It was all over the blogs, leaked to them by a secret source. Anyway, Zac wanted to rectify his bad deeds by proposing to Mystique. While he didn't confirm or deny any of the rumors, he definitely proved his love for her. And at the end of the day, that was the only thing that really mattered to Mystique.

Sam steps out on the landing and holds his arm out to me, since we're to descend the spiral staircase together as best man and maid of honor. I take in a deep breath and let it out slowly. I know that this is Mystique's idea of playing peacemaker and getting me and Sam back together, but it will be a miserable, epic fail.

He whispers as I approach, "You look beautiful, Sunday."

I don't respond, not even with a thank-you. His deception is too new, and honestly I can't even bear being in the same space as him. I am not swayed by how handsome he looks in his tuxedo or how incredible he smells. Because all of that is crushed by how he played me. It's crazy how someone can stop being attractive to you all at once when they break your heart.

We walk down the stairs arm in arm, me with a fake

smile plastered on my face, and Sam giving head nods and grins to people taking pictures. I don't think there's ever been a moment in my life that I wanted over quicker than this stroll to the altar. Sam seems to be enjoying it though.

Finally, Sam and I separate and go to opposite sides of the altar. He stands behind Zac the Zillionaire, and I wait patiently with the three other bridesmaids for Mystique to descend the stairs.

A collective gasp rises from the room as Mystique finally emerges at the top of the steps. She looks breathtaking in her white gown, accented with lace and a bodice covered in crystals. She reminds me of a Disney princess as she glides down the stairs holding on to her father's arm. This is my first time seeing him, because he and Ms. Layla aren't married, and he's not around much.

As she approaches the altar, Mystique scans the room taking in her guests, and her eyes stop on the Reign Records crew. A very brief and almost unnoticeable twitch of her nose and eyes let me know that Mystique was furious about the all white, as I knew she would be. It was probably Dreya's idea to cause her trademark drama or to do something to take away from Mystique's day. Dreya hates Mystique just enough to do that.

Although I don't have proof, I believe that Dreya is the one who leaked the story about Zac's love child to every blogger in the Internet world who even cares about black celebrities. I have no idea how she would know about the love child, but I can't think of anyone else who dislikes Mystique enough to do that.

Dreya's dislike of Mystique hinges on hatred, and not

in the fake hateration thing that artists do to one another, I mean the literal goes-down-deep hatred. That kind of feeling only can come from jealousy, and Dreya's got lots of that too. She's so envious of Mystique's success that she can't even see how talented she is in her own right.

Luckily, Mystique and Zac haven't picked a long-winded preacher to do their ceremony. These heels she's got me wearing with this dress are beyond cute, but as far as standing up goes, I think my feet are staging a mini-protest.

After they say their vows, swap kisses, and wave to their friends, family, and supporters, we are whisked away to do a Mystique and Zac wedding-day photo shoot. Of course, it's not going to be like a regular wedding where you take a bunch of pictures in about an hour and every-body goes to the reception. Oh, no. This one has hair and makeup (as if we didn't JUST do hair and makeup), and costume changes for the bride and groom.

While we're waiting for Mystique to be perfectly posed for her singular bride portrait, Sam strolls over to where I'm standing. This irritates me, because I can't find an ac-ceptable escape route, and he knows that I don't want to talk to him.

"Hey, Sunday," he says as if we are not ex-boyfriend and ex-girlfriend. "The wedding was nice, huh?"

I nod. "It was very nice."

"So, you gonna dance with me at the reception?"

Big, gigantic sigh. "Sam, I do not like you. What part of that do you not understand?"

"The not-liking part. Sunday, don't tell me you're never going to forgive me."

I scrunch my face into a twisted frown. "This has nothing to do with forgiveness. This has to do with what makes sense and what doesn't. It doesn't make sense for me to be your girlfriend, because you don't know how not to cheat."

"Based on your definition of cheating."

"My definition matches about ninety-eight percent of the entire rest of the world's definition."

Sam cracks his neck and then his knuckles. Signs that he's frustrated. Am I the one frustrating him? Really? He should practice some soul searching, and maybe he'd be irritated with himself for messing up a really good thing.

"Once you make your mind up, there's no convincing you. Rielle is a bird that goes to my mother's church. She's nothing to me."

I shake my head. "She's nothing. That's sad. I hate that she gave her virginity to you, because you keep saying that she's nothing. What type of dude are you, Sam? I mean, don't you think you could try to get back with me without crapping on Rielle?"

"There's a chance that we could get back together?"

"Nah, playa. Not even a little, slim chance."

Do you ever feel like the same drama is so tired and so played, that you don't even want to entertain it anymore? That's how I feel about Sam and our on-again, off-again relationship. It's like, come on, can I get to the next track on the CD of my life? This dude keeps trying to press replay and I'm done.com.org.info.

When the guys are taking a group shot with Zac, Mystique loops her arm in mine and smiles. "It's almost over. The day, I mean. I'm so ready for it to be done."

"Really? It's your wedding day. It's supposed to be the best day of your life."

She shrugs. "It is, but I can't help but think about Zac's child. He's the whole reason we're getting married, and that is annoying no matter how I look at it."

I glance around and notice that there's no one standing near us while we talk. Mystique is an ultra-private person, so her sharing this little tidbit out in the open is totally unlike her.

"I think that's only part of the reason, Mystique. Don't you think Zac really loves you too?"

"Of course. I wouldn't have said yes if I didn't believe that. I just think he would've stayed in single baller status with beautiful chick by his side for a while longer. The whole illegitimate child thing forced his hand."

"He's just trying to keep you from leaving him, I think. He loves you and wants you to know that you mean more than a jump-off."

She cocks her head to one side as if she hasn't considered this before. "Maybe you're right."

"I am right!" I reply. "This is not just about sending a message to the fans, but he's also saying something to the baby's mama. It doesn't matter if she does have a child with him, you are number one."

Mystique smiles and gives me a one-armed hug. "I see why everybody wants to be your friend, Sunday. You've always got the best advice."

This makes me laugh out loud. "Everybody is not trying to be my friend! I think Dreya and Bethany can pretty much do without me right now."

"Bethany was just upset for a minute, with that pregnancy thing. She was stupid to get pregnant by Dilly. He's just a baby. I don't agree with the abortion, but she did what she felt she had to do."

"She said she had a miscarriage."

Mystique shakes her head. "Nah. She had an abortion. Evan made sure of that. He heard those finished tracks off her album, and he *convinced* her to get rid of her baby."

"You say that like she wasn't really feeling it."

"She wasn't, but you know Bethany. More than anything she wants to blow up. And Reign Records was not about to promote a pregnant singer."

"That whole thing is messed up though. I hope it's worth it to her."

The guys all put on sunglasses and strike a pose with their arms folded across their chests. It's really cute, although I exclude Sam from my mind when I think of the hotness. He's not hot to me, no matter what he does.

"I know they think they're getting to me by wearing white to my wedding," Mystique says nonchalantly. "But I don't care."

This makes me chuckle. She definitely cares, but is classy and spiteful enough to not ever let Evan and his crew know that she does.

"Okay, Mystique. You know you can be real with me, right? It would piss me off what they did, so it's okay for you to be angry. I won't tell anyone."

Mystique lifts an eyebrow and flips her wig out of her face. "I am elevated so high above those haters that it doesn't even matter, seriously."

"Whatever you say, girl. Whatever you say." I give Mystique my straight face stare, to let her know that whatever it is she's selling, I'm not buying.

When we get done with the photo shoot, we enter the reception area, where everyone is already seated and nibbling on appetizers and sipping champagne. DeShawn is sitting with my mother and aunt, and apparently he's charming the heck out of my mother because she is holding her chest and giggling. She's pretty hard to impress, so I'm surprised that DeShawn has her attention.

He's got my attention too. His three-piece, fitted navy-blue suit makes him look classy enough to walk a runway. His wavy low fade, dark eyebrows and light goatee have got plenty of girls in the room checking him out. This is cool with me too, though, because DeShawn is not my man, even though he wants to be.

He's been pushing up hard, ever since we met. I told him that I had a boyfriend, and although he wasn't disrespectful with it, he still let it be known that he was ready to slide in as soon as Sam messed up. When he starred in one of my music videos, we got closer, as friends, and he's a solid member of my college clique. He even tried to help when Sam and I broke up, by bringing me some of my favorite comfort food.

All in all, DeShawn is good people, and he's going to make someone a really good boyfriend. Just not me.

I sit at the head table with the bridal party, unfortunately next to my nemesis, Sam.

"So, I have some tracks that I want you to listen to, for Dreya's album. Should I email them to you, bring them to the studio, what?"

"Eww, you smell like weed, Sam. What did you do? Smoke some after we took the pictures?"

Sam sucks his teeth. "Sunday, I told you I wasn't going to smoke weed anymore, but you know, my boys do, so it is what it is."

"Who are you?"

"I'm the same dude you met a year ago and fell for, Sunday. I'm just a lot richer."

"You are not the same dude I met, Sam. But whatever, send the tracks by email, or give them to Big D. I'll go in the studio and see if there's anything I can work with."

"You are determined to make this difficult, huh?"

I shake my head with sheer irritation. "This would not be difficult at all, if you get it through your head that we are not going to get back together. I'm all about getting this music done, so let's just do that."

Thank God Mystique's mom stands up to toast the couple, because Sam is getting on my last nerve.

Ms. Layla says, "Mystique and Zac are a perfect team. They are not just the king and queen of the industry right now, but they are a couple completely in love. They have proven today that nothing can break them down. Not bloggers, not rumors, not haters, and not jump-offs. Cheers to the happy couple!"

I hold up my glass of champagne, and watch Mystique's expression. She's smiling, but there's something that looks like uncertainty too.

The music starts, and Mystique and Zac have their first dance to "You Make me Feel Brand New." It's an old school song, but the dance is beautiful. Zac stares into

Mystique's eyes like she's the only other person in the room. He may have messed up, but he definitely loves her above all others.

After the couple's first dance, and Mystique's dance with her dad, the members of the bridal party have to dance with each other. I steel myself against how irritating it's going to be to dance with Sam.

He walks over to me purposefully, with a half smile on his face. "I know you aren't feeling this," he whispers. "But it's for Mystique and Zac."

I nod. "That's the only reason why I'm doing it."

It's a slow song, but I keep enough space between my body and Sam's that it actually looks awkward.

"You want to just hand dance?" he asks. "I know you don't want to be hugged up with me right now."

"Or ever. Let's hand dance."

Sam takes my hands and pulls me close then we separate and do a little spin. It's old school—the way our parents dance, and if I wasn't trying to hold vomit down from having to look at Sam, I might be having fun with it.

After that five-minute ordeal is over, the female members of the bridal party have a special surprise. We, along with Mystique, have choreographed a dance to "Ride" by Ciara. Everyone is entertained by our dropping it like it's hot and gyrating our hips.

I notice while we're dancing, that Sam has taken a seat next to my mother. I watch him hug her and kiss her on the cheek and chat it up for the entire song. He soooo doesn't know me if he thinks he can get back with me by going through my mother.

After the song is over, I go to DeShawn's seat and say, "Come on, I want you to meet my mother. She's met all my other college friends."

His eyes light up. "Sunday, I've already met her! I was sitting with her and your auntie."

"I know, but I didn't introduce you."

"Well, fine. But don't you think it's a little early for introductions? I mean, we haven't officially started dating yet, Sunday."

I give a little irritated head shake and pull DeShawn over to my mom. "Hey, Mommy. Are you having fun?"

"I-I guess. All this is a bit much. I'm not used to all this. Most of the weddings I go to have the reception in the church social hall."

My aunt Charlie cuts in. "This is how we are gonna live from here on out, Shawn! You wait until Dreya marries that Evan. We're gonna do it even bigger than this!"

I don't burst my aunt's bubble by telling her that there's probably no chance that Evan and Dreya will ever get married. She's obviously got a fantasy about it, so I'ma just let her go ahead and have it.

"Mommy, I just want you to meet my friend DeShawn. He's my date tonight. He plays ball at Georgia State."

My mom smiles at him. "Oh, we've already met! I thought you were one of these artists or actors or somebody. I didn't know you were one of Sunday's college friends."

DeShawn shakes my mother's hand by covering her hand with both of his. She seems to like the sincere gesture. "I am a model, Ms. Tolliver, but I'm nowhere near celebrity status like anybody here. The only reason I got on the guest list is because of Sunday."

My mother pulls me down and whispers, "He's fine. Too fine. Be careful."

I let out a little chuckle at my mother's frank observation. DeShawn is incredibly fine. It almost comes with the territory that a guy this good looking would be a player. My mom knows a little something about pretty boys too. Her last serious boyfriend, Carlos, was really good looking and even though he was faithful, he was nothing but trouble.

Now it's time to open up the dance floor to everyone and the party really starts. Of course, with my cousin and auntie in the room, the party getting started means the drama is set to pop off. Dreya picked Drama as her stage name, and she tries, every day, to live up to it.

Dreya pulls Evan to the middle of the dance floor, and starts dancing and taking pictures of them on the floor with her cell phone. Mystique has asked that no one take any pictures during the wedding or reception, especially with cell phones.

"Reign Records in the house!" Dreya shouts out when the DJ plays one of her singles.

Evan joins in, "Reign Records run this mutha! If you a Reign Records artist, you need to get out on this dance floor and represent!"

I hesitate, because even though I am a Reign artist, I know this whole display is bothering Mystique. She walked away from the whole Reign Records team and decided to stay with the parent company, Epsilon Records. Evan looked at Mystique's decision as some sort of betrayal, but Mystique and Zac did it to let Evan know he wasn't in charge of Mystique's career.

Dilly grabs my hand and pulls me to the dance floor. Even though we've had a rocky past with his brother being partially responsible for my mom's boyfriend getting shot, we are friends now. Dilly is an incredible rapper, and I want to see him blow up. He's magic on stage with me and with anyone he performs with.

"This is a baller's wedding, right?" Dilly asks as he pops and locks to the music.

I match some of his dance moves, but not all; I'm not the greatest dancer. "It is a baller's wedding! But Mystique and Zac have crazy capital."

"One day, I'ma be paid like this. I'm gonna have steak and lobster at my wedding reception."

"Yes, you are, Dilly. But a wedding for you is a long way off. You haven't even graduated from high school yet."

Dilly laughs out loud. "You love reminding me how young I am. I think you just do it to keep your feelings for me in check."

I punch Dilly lightly on the arm. "I don't have any feelings for you, boy."

"It's okay, you can admit it," Dilly says. "And I'm gonna let you have your way with me on my prom night."

"I thought you were looking for another girl to go to prom with!"

Dilly shakes his head. "That was when you were dating Sam, and he was tripping. Now he's not telling you what to do, so I want the American Music Award winner to go to my prom."

"By the time of your prom, I'm a have some Grammys too," I say with a giggle.

"All right then, Grammy winner. I'll take that too."

DeShawn steps to us. "Dude, can I get a dance in with my date?"

Dilly throws his hands up. "You get rid of one dude and scoop up another, huh? You're still going to my prom, even if this hardhead is your new boo."

"DeShawn is my friend, Dilly, so you still have a prom date."

Dilly seems satisfied with this and bounces off to dance with another pretty girl who's standing next to the dance floor. I almost thought he was going to ask Bethany, but I should've known better than that. Dilly and Bethany have too much history.

"So this is how the rich and famous get married, huh?" DeShawn asks.

I shrug in time to the music. "I guess."

DeShawn smoothly wraps one arm around my waist and takes my hand. It's a mid-tempo Mystique cut, not a slow song, but DeShawn is sure making it feel like one. I catch Sam glare over in our direction, which completely annoys me. He doesn't get to be mad about me and De-Shawn. Even if I had moved on already, which I haven't, Sam doesn't get to have any emotional meltdowns about it. He had his chance.

He. Blew. That.

DeShawn says, "So, did I tell you how much I appreciate you inviting me to this? I've got about fifteen business cards, and I got invited to do a video shoot next month. Good looking out."

I beam a smile at him. His mood is so good that it's contagious. "I'm so glad to hear that, DeShawn! Got to pay that tuition, right?"

"Yes, ma'am. You hooked a bruvah up, for real."

"Bruvah?"

"You like? I'm practicing my British accent. I might need it for one of my projects."

I laugh out loud. "Okay, boo. You might end up being the first black James Bond or something."

"I like the way you said that."

"What?"

"Okay, boo," DeShawn says. "You called me boo. I can roll with that."

"I didn't mean it like *that*, DeShawn! I just . . . well . . . never mind. Nothing I say is going to convince you that I don't want you to be my boo."

"You're right, Sunday. Because you do want me to be your boo. You just don't know it yet."

DeShawn spins me around and wraps his arms around me from behind. I must admit I'm enjoying this attention, but it's really not fair because most of my pleasure comes from the fact that Sam is about to lose his mind. Good.

"How long are you planning to keep me out?" De-Shawn asks. "I have to get in at a respectable time, you know. I'm a student."

"We can leave now, if you want. I think they're just gonna eat some cake and call it a night."

Just when I think this wedding is going to be a peaceful

affair and all love, hugs, kisses and bunnies, the drama hits the fan.

"Who in the world is that?" DeShawn asks.

The *who* he's referring to is a totally random chick who just stepped into the reception dressed like a video vixen-slash-stripper. She's got on a silver halter half top that bares her belly button and a pair of nearly sheer leggings. Does she realize that it is wintertime outside? I'm surprised she doesn't have an icicle hanging off her belly button. Her body is enough to make all of the men in the room catch their breath. Even DeShawn squeezes my hand a little tighter as if he has no control over it.

The scene-stealing chick has with her a little boy, about two or three years old. The second question after who is she, is how did she get into this reception, 'cause I dang sure can tell from the looks on Mystique's and Zac's faces that she was not on the invite list.

It's almost like time stops as she strides across the room with wide open steps, practically dragging the baby, who is trying to take twenty steps to one of hers. Zac's jaw drops when the girl stops directly in front of him and Mystique, who are walking around to all of the guest tables thanking people for coming. Everyone and everything is silent. You can hear a pin drop in the room. The DJ even stops spinning his record.

"Why wouldn't you want your son to be at your wedding, Zac?" the girl bellows at the top of her lungs.

It's clear now the answer to question number one. This chick must be the alleged baby mama whose existence actually made Zac pop the question to Mystique. I take one side-eyed glance at my cousin, and the satisfied smirk on her face gives me the answer to question number two. She may not have let the girl in ('cause she hasn't left her seat), but she must've given the girl the wedding reception venue.

Mystique's face contorts into an evil snarl. It actually scares me a little bit, even though it's not directed toward me.

"Get her out of here, Zac. Right now."

The girl laughs in Mystique's face. "You don't have to get me out of here! I will leave willingly. I just thought that Zac would want his son to be a part of his big day. You can't erase him, Zac. And you can't erase me. But as long as you keep sending me those checks, you don't have to worry about me being too much of a problem."

The girl turns to leave, but does not take the boy's hand.

"Aren't you forgetting someone, Nya?" Zac asks.

"Nope. You can arrange for a sitter when you go on your honeymoon, but I think it's time for Zac Jr. to spend some quality time with his daddy."

"You c-can't just do this!" Mystique protests.

Nya ignores Mystique and the little boy as he starts to whimper. She strides right out of the reception hall as disruptively as she came in.

The poor little boy is in full-fledged scream mode. "Mommy! Mommy!"

All those years of taking care of my little cousin Manny has given me a bit of experience in the diffusing of tears in little boys. I let DeShawn go and run to the little tot and scoop him up in my arms.

"Hey, little man!" I say as his screams turn back to whimpers. "This is a party for your daddy! You like parties?"

The little boy nods.

"Well, this is a big ol' party too! They have all kinds of cookies and cakes over there on that table. You want to get some?"

"Cake?" he asks, his tears almost forgotten.

"Yep! As much as you can eat."

I glance over at Zac and Mystique and mouth, *I got this.* I take little baby Zac over to the table and let him fill up a plate of every goodie imaginable. Then, I take him to the table where Zac and Mystique's mothers are sitting.

Zac's mother, Ellie, reaches out to the Zac Jr. "Come sit on granny's lap, baby."

A huge smile bursts onto the boy's face. He definitely recognizes his grandmother, although he doesn't seem too familiar with his daddy. He scrambles onto Ellie's lap and takes bites out of each of his desserts.

Zac signals to the DJ to start the music back up, and the party resumes as if the interruption had never occurred. I take DeShawn by the hand and walk over to Dreya and Evan's table, the Reign Records table.

I sit down in an empty seat next to Dreya. She snickers like she already knows what I'm going to say.

"That was foul," I whisper in her ear.

She shrugs. "I have no idea what you're talking about."

"That little scene. I know you had something to do with that."

Dreya laughs and runs her hand lovingly down Evan's

arm. "Sunday, I wish I had coordinated that. That chick was the most entertaining part of this bougie, boring wedding reception."

"Sunday, I know you don't think Dreya would do something like that to a label mate," Evan says. "That would just be in poor taste."

I roll my eyes at Evan because his words are saying one thing, but the glint in his eye tells me he and Dreya were probably in cahoots on this thing.

Bethany, who is sitting in the next seat, taps my arm. "Hey, girl. I didn't get a chance to speak to you earlier. You look really pretty as a bridesmaid."

"Thank you. You look good too. You ready to get back in the studio?"

She grins. "Of course. You?"

"Maybe. Gotta figure out how to navigate around Sam, but other than that I'm ready."

DeShawn leans over and takes my hand. "I can help you navigate around Sam. Like right now, I can take you right up out of here, and we can have our own after-party back at your dorm."

"I am ready to go, DeShawn, but don't think something is gonna pop off. This ain't prom night or nothing. You can eat ice cream and brownies with me and my girls if you want."

DeShawn smirks. "If that's all I can get for now, I'll take it. But pretty soon, you'll want me. You won't be able to help yourself."

This makes me laugh out loud. "Boy, if you don't take me home . . ."

"What? What's gonna happen, Sunday Tolliver? Nothing. And you know why? 'Cause you like me."

DeShawn winks at me and holds his arm out for me to grab, and he walks me right up out of Mystique and Zac's celebrity nightmare of a wedding. After this bananas day, I can't wait to get back to the calm peacefulness of my dorm at Spelman and my homegirls Gia and Piper.

3

_____

"So the wedding was bonkers?" Piper asks as she tries on a pair of my boots. They don't suit her.

We're in Gia's and my dorm, getting ready to go to a Gamma Phi Gamma party. It's the first sorority party of the semester, and since both Piper and Meagan are determined to be Gamma girls, Gia and I have no choice but to get dragged to all of their parties.

"Yeah, I'm glad the whole wedding thing is over. Mystique is a stepmama though. I think Zac's baby mama left their son with them."

"That is sooo what happened on that Tina Turner movie," Gia says as she looks at her asymmetrical afro in the mirror. "Remember? Tina had to raise Ike's kids just like they were her own."

"That's too much drama," Piper says. "If that's what being rich and famous is all about, I'll pass."

"Thanks a lot," I reply. "Since I'm on the road to

riches and fame, I hope my journey is not like Mystique's."

Gia giggles and pulls on a snug wool skirt. "You've already got stuff popping off with you, girl. DeShawn was your date, and you were in the wedding party with Sam. I just knew we were gonna get a YouTube sensation out of that situation right there."

"Sam knows what it is, plus me and DeShawn are not even all like that."

Piper says, "You are not all like that toward DeShawn, but he's definitely getting gone over you."

I groan and throw myself onto my bed and a pile of clothes. "I'm so not feeling that at all. I need a break from boys. Sam has messed it up for their gender right now."

"Who could ever get tired of boys?" Piper asks.

Before Gia or I can answer her question, there's a knock on the door. We already know that it's Meagan, because she texted us to say she was on her way. When Gia opens the door, Meagan steps in with a huge smile on her face.

"How do I look, y'all?"

Meagan is wearing head-to-toe turquoise and white, the Gamma Phi Gamma colors. She's got on a turquoise half jacket, white shimmery tank, and turquoise skinny jeans. She finishes the ensemble with silver boots.

Piper's eyes widen. "Aren't they gonna be mad if you wear their colors and you haven't crossed?"

"I am legacy," Meagan says. "For me, crossing over is a formality."

Gia lifts an eyebrow and says, "Usually, I don't agree

with Piper, but this time I think you should change. Remember there are those two chicks in the sorority who already aren't feeling you. You don't want to make anybody mad."

Meagan looks as if she's considering Gia's advice. "Maybe you're right. I don't want to start any mess. It's a new year so maybe they'll let bygones be bygones."

"We'll wait for you while you go and change," I say. "But hurry up. The party started an hour ago. I like fashionably late, but dang."

As Meagan dashes out of the room to go and change her outfit, Gia uses this as an opportunity to beef up her accessories.

"If you add one more bangle, you're gonna sound like a set of wind chimes walking up in there," Piper says.

"I like to jingle when I walk," Gia says with a laugh. "I sound musical, like Jill Scott or somebody."

"Wow" is the only response I can muster. It's hard to have a comeback for some of Gia's witticisms.

"Hey, y'all, I was thinking of picking up a couple of classes at Morehouse this semester," Piper says. "I'm thinking it will be a good way to meet guys."

Gia giggles, "So do it, but don't tell Meagan. She'll do it with you."

"I know."

"Oh, I know what I forgot to tell y'all about," Gia says in an excited tone.

"What?" I ask. I don't like the sound of the excitement. She's too amped.

"Well, you know we're having a Martin Luther King

Jr. Day celebration over in the Sisters Chapel, right?" Gia asks.

I nod. "Of course. The guest speaker this year graduated from Spelman in the sixties. I bet she marched with Dr. King."

"Right," Gia says. "So we've been asked . . . well, I've been asked to choreograph an expression of dance for the program. I thought we'd do a theatrical interpretation of 'Ride On, King Jesus.' "

I give Gia a big, blank, wide-eyed stare, trying to figure out what this has to do with me.

Piper asks, "So, you need us to help you with it?"

"I'd love for y'all to be in it. Sunday, if you do it, I know I'll get more participation from the girls on campus."

"Why does no one believe or understand me when I say that dancing is not my thing?" I ask.

"I know, I know, but I have an idea for you," Gia says. "I want you to start off singing the song solo, and then the gospel choir will join in with you. You won't have to dance at all. The dancers will do all that."

"Am I going to get to dance?" Piper asks.

"You may audition for me," Gia says. "This is going to have a lot of African dance techniques. If you don't know the moves already, it'll be hard for me to get you up to speed."

Piper rolls her eyes, jumps up from the bed, and gives us a thirty-second rendition of some African-inspired dance. If it wasn't for her pale skin, light eyes, and pointy nose, I would swear that girl was brought up on the coast of Ghana the way she swiveled her hips and swung those arms back and forth.

She's a bit out of breath when she gets done, but she says, "You mean *those* techniques?"

Gia and I burst into laughter. "All right, girl," Gia says. "You been watching a lot of *National Geographic*, Janet Jackson videos, or something, because that was on point!"

"My last foster mother's church had a praise dance group. We did those moves on a song called 'Anthem of Praise.' "

"Well, you are in, girl. I like the way you move," Gia says.

Finally, Meagan reappears in less controversial wide-leg jeans, cream turtleneck and hunter-green belted vest. This outfit is a lot more conservative, and frankly more Meagan's style.

"So, style jury, am I going to start any fights with this one?" Meagan asks.

I shake my head. "Nope. You look really sophisticated. Definitely Gamma Phi Gamma material."

"So let's roll out. I'm driving, right? And the party is at the Gamma house?"

Gia nods. "Yep. Let's be out!"

As we leave our dorm, we notice quite a few girls filing out as well, probably most of them going to the Gamma Phi Gamma party. It is the most elite sorority on campus and most of the girls who want to join any sisterhood want it to be Gamma Phi Gamma.

The Gamma girls are strict too. If they invite you to

their rush activities, they expect you to make the choice immediately to go the Gamma Phi Gamma route. If a girl seems indecisive or lets another one of the sororities court her too, she can pretty much forget crossing over as a Gamma Phi Gamma girl.

Technically, they're not allowed to pledge anyone or do any hazing activities, but there is an underground pledge process that takes place. The girls who are accepted based on the intake application alone are classified as "paper" and not given the same respect as the ones who go through the pledge process.

All of this information is completely useless to me, since I have absolutely no intention of pledging or joining any sorority. But since Piper and Meagan are Gamma fanatics, I have no choice but to hear the ins and outs of getting into Gamma Phi Gamma.

The party is definitely already jumping when we arrive. Ironically, the DJ is spinning my cut "Can U See Me" when we walk into the party, as if on cue. Although the music is bumping, there aren't many people dancing. There are clumps of girls and guys talking and laughing and a few couples grinding in corners—not exactly dancing.

DeShawn waves at me from across the room, and I give him a three-finger wave in return. For some reason, he seems to think that this means "come here," because he makes his way through the crowded room to where we are.

He hugs me and lifts me off the floor as he does so. "Hey, girl. I feel like I haven't seen you in forever."

I laugh. "I just saw you at Mystique's wedding."

"Too long, too long. You could call me or text me or something," DeShawn fusses.

Gia starts clearing her throat violently. DeShawn asks, "Gia you okay?"

"Yeah," she says, "I'm just kind of *thirsty*. You know what that feels like, right?"

DeShawn rolls his eyes. "Thirsty doesn't describe me in the least. I just like what I like."

"Anyway!" Gia says. "I see my homeboy Kevin. Where's Ricky? He said he was probably gonna come through."

DeShawn shrugs. "I left him on campus. He might not have had a ride. Maybe you should go and call him."

"Anything to get rid of me, huh?" Gia asks.

DeShawn nods and smiles. "Unh-huh! Now go and find your man."

"You doing all right?" DeShawn asks as Gia rushes away, furiously pressing numbers on her cell phone.

"I am cool. Yeah, pretty cool."

"Good, because I have a question to ask you."

I feel my stomach flip. "Okay . . ."

"Did you invite me to Mystique's wedding because you really wanted me as a date, or did you just invite me to make Sam jealous?"

"I . . . uh . . . um . . . well . . ."

Thank God for Meagan and her total disregard of conversation etiquette when she has something important to say. I have absolutely no idea how to answer DeShawn's question and not sound like a jerk, so I am so happy that Meagan nearly knocks DeShawn over to get to me. The truth is, I invited him to the wedding so that I wouldn't have to deal with Sam's trying to get me back.

"What's wrong?" I ask her.

"Wrong? Nothing's wrong! Nothing at all."

"Then why the dramatic entrance?" DeShawn asks.

Meagan looks DeShawn up and down like he's the one who interrupted. Then she dismisses him with a wave of her hand. Rude, but the hilarious look on DeShawn's face is totally worth it.

"I have found him, Sunday. My husband, my Chi Kappa Psi man. My Morehouse soul mate."

"And you know this already?"

"I do, I do. He introduced himself, and he summers down the road from my family in the Hamptons. He's going to study medicine, he's deliciously fine, and he asked me out on a date. I could just pass out right now!"

"Well, what's this Romeo's name?" I ask with a little giggle. It's hard not to be tickled seeing Meagan like this. Her pin-straight hair is whipping all around as she jerks her head on that pencil-thin frame.

"His name is Linden. And I think I'm in love."

"You can't know you're in love that fast," DeShawn protests as if he is a part of the conversation.

"Does this guy know who I am?" Meagan asks.

I shake my head. "Apparently not."

Meagan is the girl with the plan. She already knows the end of her story. By the time she turns thirty, she's going to be married to a doctor from Gamma Phi Gamma's brother fraternity, Chi Kappa Psi, be mother of two kids, and own a four-bedroom house and a little dog.

Sometimes I envy her a little bit. It seems like the only thing that I'm sure of right now is that I'm going to finish college and keep pushing forward with my music. As for love . . . that has temporarily eluded me.

And I think that if it comes again, it certainly won't be planned. It's almost one-hundred-percent sure to catch me by surprise.

4

"I'm so not surprised by this," I say as Mystique pushes her tablet across the table at me to show me a YouTube video from inside her wedding. "You think Dreya did this?"

I take a long sip of my fresh-squeezed orange juice as I wait for Mystique to respond. We're at Zac's house, in the sun room, having breakfast the Wednesday after Mystique and Zac's wedding. Why can't I enjoy this gourmet prepared French toast and hash browns?

"Who else would post a video of Zac's crazy baby's mother? I swear your cousin is out to destroy me."

I consider this accusation. I wouldn't put it past Dreya to try and destroy Mystique's career, but in my opinion, it wouldn't really be a good idea. Dreya is trying to reform her image, and stay in good with the record label. Starting a little controversy is one thing, but I don't think Dreya is really trying to ruin Mystique.

"Destroying your career doesn't help her one bit. Your record sales provide revenue for the company. It's the only way Reign Records can exist."

"I know this and you know it, but does your cousin ever think before she acts? She's a one-chick catastrophe. A category-five hurricane waiting to tear up the coast."

I can't disagree, so I simply give a quick nod. "Don't worry about it, Mystique. The girl looks crazy and Zac married you. When are y'all going on your honeymoon?"

"No time soon. I've got to get to work on my new album, and I'm working with a whole new team of writers and producers."

I'm a little shocked at this news. I was sure she'd ask me to contribute some music to her next effort. The last song I gave her went straight to the top of the Billboard charts the week it was released.

"I want a different sound this time. Something to set me completely apart from what Evan is doing," Mystique explains as if she's got the ability to spy on my brain waves.

"It's all good. I've got more than I can handle right now anyway. I've got Dreya's second album to do, and we're planning my second release. With school too, I might need to clone myself to finish all of these projects."

"Bethany's record is going to solidify you in the game as a songwriter. You won't have to tour and do all the extra stuff to make money, because you'll have enough songwriting gigs to keep you busy."

"I hope so, because I can't really do a good tour right now. Not unless it's over the summer months."

"Speaking of a summer tour, I think I want you to open for me at some of my European shows this summer. I'm talking Paris, Monaco, London, Madrid, and maybe even Lisbon."

Even though my life has been on warp speed since my senior year of high school, summer seems so far away. It's only January now, and I've got a whole other semester in college to worry about.

"It sounds like a great opportunity," I say.

"But . . ."

"But nothing! Why do you think there's a but?" I ask.

"Because your body language tells me you're not feeling it."

"I'm just stressed out right now, girl. I hope that I get to go on the tour with you."

Mystique lifts an eyebrow as if she doesn't believe me. "Okay, Sunday. I'm gonna let that slide. I noticed that you and Sam didn't have a reunion at the wedding."

I laugh out loud. "I know you didn't think that was going to happen. He should've brought a date so he didn't look so lonely."

"Girl, you are harsh. And you brought DeShawn with you? That had to be uncomfortable. Do they know each other?"

"They met when we went to Destin, a couple months ago. But Sam and I were still together then, so it didn't really matter."

"I wish my drama was as uncomplicated as yours. I've got a child running around my house that doesn't belong to me."

"Are you serious? I just thought she was doing that for show and that she would come back and get her baby. Who does that?"

"A trifling, deadbeat skank. She'll be back though, because Zac's been paying her child support for two years. I guarantee she doesn't want that gravy train to stop."

"What if she doesn't come back? Are you ready to be a stepmother?"

Now it's Mystique's turn to laugh. "I guess. With the help of round-the-clock nannies. I'm not even gonna act like I'm the domestic type. I don't know what to do with a toddler. I did play with dolls, but they were never babies. They were always grown-up girls in a singing group. I played *Dreamgirls* with my dolls."

All of this happening with Mystique and Zac helps solidify my decision to stay away from Sam. I don't think this stuff with Rielle was totally random. This is one of those a-ha moments, my mother always like to talk about. She would say that God was trying to tell me something. I just hope I can slow down long enough to hear Him.

5

Evan Wilborn, the head of our record label, Reign Records, is in lecture mode. Bethany, Dilly, Dreya a.k.a. Drama, and I are sitting like ducks in a row in Big D's studio, while Big D sits back quietly. It's not like him to be silent—he's our manager. But I think the more that Evan steps to the forefront, the more Big D plays the background.

"Drama and Sunday, I know y'all are gonna bring home at least one Grammy for Reign Records. It'll be our first."

Dreya gives me a sly glance out the corner of her eye. We're both nominated for Best New Artist, and I'm nominated for Song of the Year for "Can U See Me."

Dreya didn't make it a secret that she's jealous of my nominations. She told my mom that she hopes I lose, because I don't deserve to get any awards until she's had her time to shine. She's got it twisted.

We haven't really spoken much since I had a Thanksgiving meltdown after I found out Dreya tried to get me dropped from the record label. Dreya was pretty heated at our holiday dinner too, because she found out that I'm a millionaire now, and her cash flow is severely limited. Plus, she's moved in with Evan in New York City, so I barely ever get to see her.

"Bethany and Dilly, I'm glad that the two of you are able to put your differences aside to perform your single. Actually, the fact that all of you have been asked to perform is an incredible win."

"We're going to be in the Grammy pre-show, though. Nobody even watches that," Dilly says.

"That's the exact opposite of the attitude you should have!" Evan roars. "Every time you take the stage you should look at it like your chance to gain a new fan. Don't ever let me hear you dog an opportunity again."

Sufficiently checked, Dilly lowers his head and stares at the floor. "Chin up!" Evan says. "Don't ever let anyone take the wind out of your sails like that."

Dilly snaps his head back up with a confused look on his face. He's not the only one who doesn't understand Evan, though. We're all pretty befuddled.

"What about my sophomore album?" Dreya says. "You said we were gonna talk about that, right, babe?"

Evan's nose flares a bit. I can't decipher if the look is irritation or anger, but I can tell that he doesn't like being interrupted when he thinks he's on a roll.

"I did say we would talk about your album. So let's do that right now. Sunday, Drama says you aren't exactly motivated to work on her new songs."

"I'm not motivated to do anything at all for Dreya's career."

Big D says, "Sunday, regardless of how you feel right now about your cousin, working on her record is just more money in the bank for you. Don't let somebody else get your paper."

"And I'm even willing to get some new producers," Evan says, "since you seem to be having some issues with Sam as well."

"I've figured out a way to collaborate with Sam without seeing him. I'll send him my vocals, and he can build the tracks around them."

"I want y'all in the lab together like y'all did on Bethany's stuff," Dreya says. "Y'all gave her a hot album."

I shake my head. "Not happening. Send me some other producers to the lab if you want, but there's no way I'm going to be in the same room with Sam."

"What if I give you bonus points on the album?" Evan asks.

I lift an eyebrow and ponder this. Evan is speaking my language—Benjamins. "How many extra?"

"Enough to add to your already substantial stash of loot."

I run my fingers over the crown medallion on my neck, the Reign Records symbol. "Okay. I'll do it. I won't like it, but if y'all are convinced that Sam and I have to be joined at the hip to write music, I'll do it. But he has to work around my schedule."

"You always have to be in control, don't you?" Dreya asks. "You were like that when we were in Daddy's Little Girls, and now you're trying to do it with my album."

"Wait. What is Daddy's Little Girls?" Evan asks.

Evan met us after we'd become solo artists with Big D. Obviously, he doesn't know that Dreya, Bethany, and I started off as a group, and that I wrote the songs and did all of the vocal arrangements.

Bethany says, "We used to be a girl group. It seems like such a long time ago, but it was only last year."

"Sing something," Evan says.

"Hip Hop Bugle Boy, in one, two, three, four, five, six, seven . . ."

We bust out the harmonies on En Vogue's popular song, like we were the ones who made it famous. The runs are perfect, the ad libs are perfect, and every note is totally on pitch. We were always a good group when Dreya actually opened her mouth up to sing.

"That was hot," Evan says. "Y'all should consider doing a few songs together."

Dreya sucks her teeth and frowns. "I don't even think so. I am a solo artist. Period. Girl groups ain't hot."

"Think of it as your gimmick. Reign Records's gimmick." Evan paces the room tapping his chin in thought. "Every time a Reign Records artist releases an album, there should be a group collaboration."

"Well, what about me?" Dilly asks. "I'm a Reign Records artist."

"You could rap on whatever track they do."

I shake my head. "I want to keep my brand separate from Dreya. She's not really all that positive, and I'm getting covers of teen magazines."

"Think about it!" Bethany says. "It would be a way for each of us to cross-promote our records to each other's fan bases. And no one in the industry right now can hit harmonies like us."

"Big D, what do you think?" Evan asks.

Big D chuckles. "Really? You want my opinion?"

"Don't be a diva," Dreya says. "Tell us what you think."

After a long, pregnant, diva-like pause, Big D says, "I think it is a really good idea. It will help all four of you move a lot more units, and that is the point, isn't it?"

"That's what's up! There will be Reign Records group collaborations on every record that's released. As we gain more artists, the collaborations will get bigger." Evan claps his hands together and does a half skip over to the keyboard. He sits down at the bench and bangs out a short tune.

What just happened? Did my career just step into the let's-go-backward time machine? It was cool singing with Dreya and Bethany, but I've moved beyond this. I know exactly what my mentor, Mystique, would say.

"Don't do it. Evan is an idiot," Mystique says as we have lunch at her favorite sushi bar. I am not a fan of sushi. I'd much rather be eating chicken and waffles or some macaroni and cheese, but Mystique always picks when we eat out.

I nod in agreement. "I mean, we sounded great together. We always have. But Dreya and I are not in a good place. The only reason I agreed to even work on her record is because Evan offered me extra points."

"He did? He must be desperate for her record to be a hit. You're hot right now."

I shrug. "Thing is, I can't work when I'm not inspired. I'm not a machine. I don't like Sam and I can barely stand to look at Dreya without choking her. Plus, I've got exams coming up soon. I don't know how to find my writing place."

"You need to go on some dates. Have some fun. What about DeShawn?" Mystique says. "He'd be a lot of fun, right?"

I bite my lip and consider DeShawn. Everything about him is perfect, except the fact that he's not Sam. As much as Sam is on my list of least favorite people right now, I think he might've been my first love.

A huge knot forms in my throat as I think about the fun Sam and I had in Barbados. It was the most fun I've ever had in my life. I'd never take back anything about us. If only he'd been faithful.

I think I'm heartbroken.

"I-I'm not ready for fun, Mystique."

She reaches across the table and places her hand over mine, an uncharacteristically caring gesture. It almost doesn't feel genuine, but I don't care, because I could use the sympathy, even if it is fake. Her touch seems to pop the cork off of a boatload of unshed tears. I thought I was done crying over Sam, but apparently, I'm not.

"You know, Sam really wants you back," Mystique says. "He was just telling Zac how much he misses you and how much he messed up."

"He was?"

Mystique nods. "Yes, he was. But you're not going to fall for it. You're going to ignore the pain you're feeling."

"I am?"

"Yes. I thought I wanted you two to get back together, but after this fiasco with Zac's baby's mother, I'm totally against unhealthy relationships, and you and Sam were totally unhealthy. He had his opportunity to do the right thing and he didn't. His loss."

She hands me a tissue from her purse and then waits patiently while I dry my tears and blow my nose.

"I agree with you about Sam," I say. "It was unhealthy, and he told me more lies than he did truth. But I disagree about DeShawn. If he wants to be my boyfriend, he's going to have to be incredibly patient. Because that's not going down anytime soon."

"He's someone to have on your arm at events. He's hot, and y'all look good together. It'll also keep the paparazzi from asking you about Sam. Even they aren't that tacky to ask about your ex in front of your new guy."

"DeShawn as my date to the Grammys?" I hadn't thought about it before, but not only would that be a great message to the reporters, it would also be a message to Sam. He'll know I'm serious about moving on if I bring DeShawn to a public red carpet event.

"Yes, and as your date to everything. No one has to know that you're not actually dating. It can be your mystery. Zac and I played games with the media for years before we ever admitted to being in a relationship."

"So, if they ask me about us, what should I say?"

Mystique grins. "Just smile and say, 'I never talk about my private life.' "

She never talks about her private life. But . . . I think that everyone's else life is totally fair game for Mystique.

6

"Spelmanites," Gia barks in her bossy voice. "Let's get this dance perfected. I will get extra credit in our ADW class if we do this right for the program."

ADW is our African Diaspora and the World class. It's mandatory for every freshman at Spelman. It's the one class I share with all of my new friends.

We've been practicing Gia's dance in the common area of our dormitory. Every time I see someone walking by, like they're going to get some rest, I envy them. Gia is ridiculous with her work ethic! I am tired.

"I'm not doing this dance," Meagan says. "It requires way too much movement, and I am sweaty and hot by the first half of the song. That isn't cute at all."

"There aren't going to be any Morehouse men at the program, Meagan," Piper says. "It's going to be just us girls."

"Are we doing this or aren't we?" I ask. "If not, I need to practice my Grammy performance."

"What are you singing?" Piper asks.

" 'The Highlight.' "

Meagan says, "What are you wearing, though? That's more important than the song. Who knows who might see you on the red carpet? It could be your fairy tale prince."

I laugh out loud. Meagan's priorities are always hilarious. It's always about how to land the husband with her.

Gia lets out a low wolflike growl. "Is this going to be a group effort or am I doing this dance solo?"

We trudge back over to our positions and go through the dance, this time managing to get through Gia's back-breaking routine without collapsing.

"Better," Gia says emotionlessly when the music stops. "Next time, maybe we'll actually look like we *know* this routine."

"Man, whatever!" Piper says. "I'm done rehearsing! I've got to study. You act like we're being paid for this performance."

"I thought y'all wanted to do everything in excellence!" There's a pleading tone in Gia's voice that makes all three of us stop for a moment.

"Come on, Gia. What are you really stressed out about?" I ask. "It can't be this dance. I mean, it's really not that serious, you know?"

Gia sighs and wipes her sweat drenched brow with a towel. "It's Ricky. I don't know what he's tripping on, but ever since that Gamma Phi Gamma party, he's been acting some kind of way toward me."

"What do you mean?" Piper asks. "Ricky is the perfect boyfriend."

"There's nothing specific," Gia says. "It's just a general feeling that we're drifting away from each other, and that there's nothing that I can do about it."

"Do you think it's another girl?" I ask. I'm hoping not, because Ricky was giving me hope that there were some good guys still left on the planet. If he's playing Gia, I won't know what to believe anymore.

"No. Ricky wouldn't do that. He would break up with me before he played me for somebody else. That's our rule."

After a long moment of silence Meagan asks, "Do you think that you'll marry Ricky?"

Gia nods. "I can't see myself without him. That would be all kinds of crazy to me if he married someone else."

"Then you should probably see what he's buggin' about," Piper says. "Don't let it sit for too long without you saying anything."

Gia packs all of her dance gear into her bag, takes a long sip of water from her water bottle, and wipes the sweat from her brow with the back of her hand. "I'm out, chickadees. Please do not forget that choreography. The Black History Month program is next week."

Piper says, "It'll be fine, Gia. If we get up there and don't remember the moves, we can always just freestyle."

"Uh, no. You cannot. Not unless you want to feel my wrath. Deuces, y'all."

Gia jogs out of the dorm's common area, dialing her phone with one hand and struggling with her bags with the other hand. She's one of the most impatient people

I've ever met. She was so in a hurry to know Ricky's malfunction that she couldn't even wait to get back in the privacy of our bedroom.

"So are we dismissed?" Meagan asks. "I'm going on another date with my Morehouse man."

"This will be the third date, right?" Piper asks.

Meagan's grin brightens her entire face, and makes her sharp features look soft and warm. "This will be the third date. After tonight I'll know if he's the one."

"What's so magical about the third date?" I ask.

"The first date is always super-duper awkward," Meagan explains. "On the second date, you're still wondering if the person is going to do something crazy. But by the third date, you both are a lot more relaxed. If we do well on this date, he is definitely husband material."

"You said he was pre-med, right?" Piper asks.

"So, what if, just for giggles we imagine that he never finishes medical school . . ."

Meagan frowns deeply. "Of course he's going to finish medical school."

"But what if he doesn't," Piper says. "What if he goes to work for a company that sells tennis balls and golf balls?"

"I would never marry a man who worked at a company like that. Maybe if he owned the company, we could talk."

Meagan continues to amaze me with her focus on getting her Morehouse dream guy. But, I guess we're somewhat alike. We're both all about goals. Mine involve my music and getting this money, and hers are all about love and marriage.

Meagan gives me and Piper her signature air kisses and leaves us sprawled on the floor. I wonder if Piper is feeling as lazy as I am. After Gia's insane workout, I don't feel like moving, even though I've got more than enough things to do. I've got so much to do that I don't know where to start.

"Are you excited about going to the Grammys?" Piper asks after taking a huge swig of water. "I noticed you didn't ask us to backup dance for you this time. Are you hiring other people?"

I stand to my feet and stretch my limbs. "I'm not having dancers. I'm singing a ballad, so it's just gonna be me onstage. We thought it would be a good way to save money on dancers, travel, and all that other stuff, you know?"

"Y'all selling millions of records, but y'all penny pinching like that?"

I don't feel like explaining to Piper how all of these expenses are subtracted from my royalties—my cash at the end of the day. And I am determined to stay paid. I haven't forgotten the miniature check Dreya got after having a hit record. That is soooo not gonna be me.

"Yes. I am a penny pincher. You see I'm still driving my Camry."

"Yeah, but you're paying off people's tuition bills."

I give Piper a half smile. I keep telling her that she doesn't have to keep thanking me for helping with her tuition bill. Her situation is kind of jacked, so I was happy to do it. It was the best thing I've done so far with my money.

"Did you get everything straightened out with your financial aid?"

She nods. "Still haven't located the mother unit, but my foster mom's lawyer was able to get me declared as financially independent. So, I should be straight as long as I keep my grades up."

"I have to keep my grades tight too," I say. "I didn't come to college just for show, but I didn't know it would be this hard."

I got a paper back from my composition class that was a C+. I don't remember the last time I got a C on anything. I remembered writing the paper. It was a marathon session, powered by Starbucks coffee after a Reign Records listening party for Bethany's album. It wasn't my best work and I wasn't proud of what I turned in. Apparently, my professor agreed.

"Yeah, it's hard," Piper agrees, "but I don't have a choice. Why you playing, I need to go study instead of sitting here with you."

"I know, right! You want any coffee? I'm gonna do a quick Starbucks run."

She shakes her head and frowns. "Ewww! No. And you need to stop drinking all that coffee."

"It's my energy source."

"If you do yoga with me in the morning, you'd have enough energy all day. You'd feel invigorated! I promise!"

My response to this is silence and a blank stare.

Piper and I part ways as she gets straight to our dorm and I rush out, looking a straight-up sweaty, hot mess.

Of course, because I'm riding the hot-mess train, I run

into DeShawn on my way to the car. From the way his eyes do a quick sweep of my non-matching dance ensemble and high fuzzy ponytail, I can tell that I look worse than I think I do.

"It's the Grammy-nominated Sunday Tolliver," De-Shawn says with a grin.

"Hopefully, soon to be the Grammy-winning Sunday Tolliver."

DeShawn gives me a fist bump in agreement. "I would hug you," he says, "but you look stankadocious."

I sniff my armpits and laugh. "Naw. I'm straight."

Then, I bumrush DeShawn with a surprise hug. His subsequent attempt to escape causes us both to erupt in a flurry of giggles.

"Speaking of the Grammys, Mystique says I should ask you to escort me to the awards show."

"Mystique says?"

"Well, she suggested."

"And you agreed with the suggestion."

"Not sure yet."

"So, why are we talking about it?" DeShawn looks genuinely confused. I guess this isn't making much sense.

I shrug. "I'm just throwing it out there, in case you're busy that weekend. So, I can, um . . . know."

DeShawn strokes his barely there goatee. "Well, if you happen to decide you agree with Mystique, I would cancel every hot date with every fine girl to escort you. It would be great for my career."

His *career*? That's why he wants to go with me?

"You do not have any hot dates," I say.

"What? You betta recognize. A modelesque brotha

like me? Why do you think I'm on the Spelman campus? I've got a study date."

The twinge of irritation I feel at DeShawn's revelation catches me completely by surprise. He smiles as he watches my reaction.

"Excuse me," I finally reply after a long pause. "I didn't realize you were so popular. It must be because of being in my video."

DeShawn staggers backward as if I've punched him. "Dang, Sunday. That was below the belt."

"I'm just sayin'."

"Where are you going anyway? Don't you know the paparazzi are lurking in the bushes waiting to get a picture of your celebutante self?"

I didn't think of this. Mystique's head would probably explode if she knew I was going out in public less than runway ready.

"I'm getting coffee. Got a date with my laptop."

"You might want to comb your hair first."

I groan. Fixing my hair will take at least an hour.

"Or," DeShawn continues, "I could pick it up for you."

"I thought you were on your way to a date. Won't she be mad that you kept her waiting?"

"Oh, I was just playing. I was coming by to see you. I haven't heard from you in a week."

I laugh out loud. "Okay, since you're coming clean, I should too. I do agree with Mystique. I'd love it if you'd be my date for the Grammys."

"You paying?"

"Of course. Well, Reign Records is paying."

"Cool. Then, I'm treating on your coffee. Venti, caramel macchiato, right?"

"Right."

"Okay, be right back."

DeShawn jogs away, but I don't move. All I have to do is wait a moment. Wait for it. . . . Okay, now he's stopped jogging. He turns around and jogs back.

"Can I borrow your car?" DeShawn asks while trying to catch his breath.

I dangle the keys in front of his face. "I wondered why you didn't ask."

"I was so pumped about going to the Grammys that I kind of forgot." He takes the keys from my hand. "I'll be back. Then we can hang."

"I gotta study."

"Okay, you study. I'll hang." DeShawn winks at me and trots off toward my car.

My heart flutters just a little bit that DeShawn was coming to visit me for no reason at all. Dang! Why do I like him totally against my will?

My head knows that I'm fresh off a breakup with Sam, and that DeShawn will most probably end up discarded like the majority of rebound guys. But, the warmth in the pit of my stomach is very real. And the anticipation of us having a good time together without the crew at the Grammys makes me feel even warmer.

I spin on one heel and skip back to the dorm. Yeah, I actually am skipping. I do believe this might be my favorite day of this week.

And it's all because of DeShawn and his *fine* self.

7

Ugh! This is the worst day I've had all week, and it's all because of Sam's irritating, cheating, weed-smoking behind.

We're in the lab, Big D's studio, the place where Sam and I have come up with most of our songwriting magic. Big D is here too, I guess to act as a referee, and to make sure that I don't scratch Sam's eyeballs out. But even Big D in all his cuddly warmth, can't make me and Sam get along. We've been snapping at each other all morning, and I'm ready to go. There are other things I can do today besides get fussed at by my ex-boyfriend.

After a third time of me singing the same line, Sam says, "Come on, Sunday, let's get this melody down. You've sung it differently each time. How can I decide how to do a track if you keep singing it different?"

Sam's tone is really getting on my nerves. "You are on

level ten right now, Sam. You need to bring it down a notch."

"You act like we've got all the time in the world to finish these songs. All you're writing on this one is a hook anyway. Dreya is rapping on this song."

I stand to my feet. "Big D, I'm sorry. I thought I could do this, but I can't."

"What you trippin' on?" Sam asks. "Oh, you can't work with me now?"

Part of me wonders how Sam is okay with this situation. Is he not the least bit upset that we aren't together? Maybe I really didn't mean all that much to him to begin with. With all the lies he's told, and games he's played, that's probably the case.

Sam's phone buzzes on the edge of his keyboard. He flips it over and hops off the bench.

"I gotta take this. Be right back."

"Who is that? Your new chick?" I ask the question before I can stop myself. I sound so jealous right now, and that is not even the case.

Sam rolls his eyes. "No. It's Zac. But what do you care anyway? I heard you're gonna be boo'ed up at the Grammys."

I roll my eyes back at Sam, ease down into my seat, and cross my arms over my chest in a huff. I'm feeling a mixture of embarrassment and fury. Big D gives me a long, concerned, fatherly gaze.

"Boo'ed up?" Big D asks. "With who? You were just with Sam at the American Music Awards. What message do you think it will send to show up with a new guy?"

"The message that Sam and I are absolutely not an item. I'm going with DeShawn."

"Model dude from the video? I bet that was Mystique's idea."

I nod. "Yeah, it was, but I happen to like DeShawn so it's all good."

"Watch Mystique," Big D says. "I feel that she doesn't want you and Sam together for selfish reasons."

"Like what? What does our relationship or lack thereof have to do with her?"

"You and Sam are a team. A darn great team. You are nominated for a Grammy on your very first project for Song of the Year. No matter how much Mystique claims to be on your side, you are a threat to her. Don't diss her or cut her loose, but don't ever forget."

Everyone keeps telling me not to trust Mystique, but the only ones that keep hurting me are the ones close to my heart. Sam's betrayal stings more than Mystique's possible jealousy at our rapid rise to fame. And my cousin Dreya tried to get me dropped from my record deal, yet I'm in the studio writing hits for her project. It sounds like there are lots of people I shouldn't trust and Mystique is the least of these.

"Me and Sam not being together has nothing to do with Mystique. He's a liar, and he played me. Plus, it wouldn't benefit Mystique for us to not be a songwriting team. We wrote a hit record for her too, remember?"

Big D shakes his head wearily. "Listen, I don't know for sure if she's out to get you. I'm just saying watch your back."

"I thought you had my back, Big D? What's up with that?"

He gives me that slow and infectious smile that makes the women forget that he weighs over three hundred pounds. "I always have your back, baby girl. Me and your mama are probably the only ones you can trust."

Sam comes back into the room and sits down on the keyboard bench. He's frowning now, but I can't bring myself to ask why.

"Since you can't seem to get the song right," Sam says, "why don't we work on our Grammy acceptance speech?"

I scrunch my nose into a grimace. I don't know why it didn't occur to me that I would have to walk up and receive the award with Sam. Song of the Year is an award for the songwriter, not the artist, so this is another moment that we'd share.

"If we win, we should just give our own separate acceptance speeches. You have different people to thank, and I mean we are two separate people."

Sam nods slowly. "Okay. By the way, I'm taking my mom to the Grammys."

"Okay . . ."

"So who are you going with?" Sam asks, but his question sounds like an accusation or a demand. He's straight-up tripping.

I look Big D straight in the eye and ask, "Who does this dude think he's talking to?"

Big D bursts into laughter. His entire body jiggles when he laughs, and his face lights up too. He loves a good joke, and I know Sam has got to be joking coming at me like that.

Sam now seems irritated by the laughter, and there's a reddish undertone to his caramel-colored skin, indicating a bit of embarrassment.

"You know what? I don't even care who you're going with. It ain't with me, so whatever," Sam says. He starts banging out chords on the keyboard like he's lost his ever-loving mind.

"Oh, calm down! I'm going with my friend DeShawn. He's not my boyfriend, so you can stop tripping."

"I saw how that dude was all on you in that video. We weren't even broken up yet. Why you talking about me playing you? It looks like you were doing some playing too," Sam says.

Okay, now I'm about to be on anger and fury level ten. I know he's not about to sit up here and accuse me of being unfaithful. Not when I was the one who was holding on to us for dear life.

"Don't do that, Sam. Do not do that."

"Don't do what? Don't throw your past dirt up in your face? Why not? That's how you do me. I can't live anything down."

"Oh my goodness! You kicked it with someone behind my back, took her virginity, and then bought her a computer! Not to mention the girl you slobbered down in the club. I haven't done anything to you, Sam."

Dreya picks this moment to bounce down the stairs and into the lab. "Ugh. Can y'all stop fighting and finish my songs?"

"I'm in agreement with Drama," Big D says. "Let's take this one song at a time. Can y'all agree to bury the hatchet for the rest of the day?"

Sam and I both tentatively nod. I don't know if I have a hatchet. It's more like a sword. But I do want to get back to my dorm. Today is the last day of the weekend, and I've got a paper to finish up for my composition class.

"Let me hear what y'all been working on," Dreya demands.

"Hold up," Big D says as his currently on-again girl-friend Shelly descends the stairs daintily carrying a tray with glasses of lemonade and slices of cake. Shelly is like the hood Martha Stewart. She's always baking or cooking something. How she does it in five-inch heels, acrylic nails, and ten pounds of hair weave, I'll never understand. She smiles at Big D like he's the only one in the room. I could never be like her. Big D plays her for sideline chicks all the time. They get into arguments, she storms out, and he begs her to come back. She always does. That is crazy to me.

"Y'all want some of this cake?" Shelly asks. Her thick Southern accent tells me that she's a native Georgia peach just like me.

"I'll pass," Dreya says. "The last thing I need is cake."

"Your body is perfect. You can eat what you want," Big D says.

Dreya shakes her head. "No. Evan told me that my skin is dull when I don't eat right. When I get off the plane in New York, I want to be glowing."

Glowing? Really? I've never seen Dreya quite so taken with a guy like she is with Evan. I think she, like Shelly, turns a blind eye and a deaf ear to dirt he might be doing. This is how rich guys get over, I guess, because girls will stay with them in spite of foolishness, just so they can get iced up with diamonds and wear designer clothes.

"When does your flight leave?" Sam asks. "Are we going back on the same flight?"

"I'm leaving next Friday," Dreya says.

"Oh, naw, then. I'm out tomorrow morning," Sam says.

"You let your man be alone that long?" Shelly asks as she sets her tray with the uneaten cake slices on the table.

"Me and my man are both grown," Dreya replies. "I'm not stressing what he does when I'm not there, just like he's not stressing what I do. That's called grown and sexy."

I roll my eyes and shake my head. "Okay, moving right along. Here's what we came up with so far. Come on, Sam. Play the music."

Sam moves slowly, like he doesn't like being bossed by me. After a long and deliberate pause, he starts to play.

I sing, "You checking up on me/You checking up on me/Who do you think you are?/You don't own me/You don't know me/I'm a star, baby/Nobody checks up on me."

Dreya squeals with delight as we finish the song. "That's hot! I love it. When can I record it?"

"We have to write the second verse, and the bridge," I say. "But it'll be next week."

"Why do we have to wait until next week? You and Sam were always able to bust out a song in an hour or so. What's up?" Dreya asks.

I'm not even going to respond to this. Dreya knows exactly what's up between me and Sam. Everyone in our camp knows. She's just being messy right now. Sam takes off his baseball cap, scratches the top of his head, and replaces it. I know what this gesture means. He's trying to avoid answering the question too. It's amazing how much I picked up of Sam's individual tics from dating him just that little short time.

"Sunday, can I talk to you in private for a minute?" Dreya asks. Then she looks at Sam, Shelly, and Big D. "Can we have a second?"

Big D frowns. "Am I being kicked out of my own studio?"

"Just for a minute," Dreya says. "I really, really need to talk to my cousin."

Okay, what is Dreya on? *My cousin?* I haven't heard her refer to me that way since we were little. She doesn't even introduce me as her cousin. She's always like, "This is Sunday."

Sam pulls his hat low on his head and stands from the keyboard. "Sunday, get at me before I leave, even if we have to finish this song over the phone."

He doesn't wait for my response, but goes upstairs two steps at a time. Shelly sets her plate of pound cake down on the table and follows behind Sam. Big D is a lot slower in getting up the stairs. I'm starting to be concerned about him. All that weight he's carrying cannot be good.

When they are safely upstairs with the door to the basement closed, Dreya says, "Sunday, I've got something to say to you. And it's gonna be hard, but I have to do it."

"Okay."

"I am sorry for what I did to you. I'm sorry I went to

Epsilon Records and tried to get you dropped from your deal."

This is a shock! An apology from Dreya? Am I being punk'd?

"Why did you do it? I still don't understand why."

"Sunday, don't you see? You are a better singer than me! You write songs. You're prettier than me! I just wanted, for once, to be better than you . . . to have something that belongs to me."

"Wow. I don't even know what to say."

"But I don't feel the same way anymore. I know that there is room for both of us."

I am skeptical of this entire conversation. This is so unlike Dreya that I think it has to be coming from someone else.

"Did Evan tell you to apologize?" I ask.

Dreya shakes her head. "No, but he did tell me I was wrong to hate on you. I thought he'd be on my side, but he wasn't. He thinks family is everything."

"So it took Evan to tell you everything my mom has been saying to you since we were little?"

Dreya looks at the floor and shrugs. When she raises her head there are tears in her eyes. "Sunday, do you know how jealous I've been of you our entire lives?"

"What?"

"You had the good mother. Auntie Shawn works hard and y'all always had someplace to stay. Me and Manny never knew where we were gonna live, or even if we'd have dinner."

I bite my lip and sadly think about Dreya's life. Aunt Charlie was always in kickin'-it mode. She partied hard, even when she needed to be there for her kids. My mom always had to bail her out and make sure my cousins had a roof over their heads. It always irritated me when they lived with us, because I didn't have my own space. I never once thought about how they felt having to live with us.

"Dreya, my mother would've never let y'all go without."

"I know, but I wanted her to be my mother. I wished like crazy that Auntie Shawn would just adopt me. My mom just wanted to have fun, and she still does. That gets old."

I inhale a deep breath and then release it. "So, I guess I have to forgive you, huh?"

Dreya bursts into laughter. "I mean, it would probably be the right thing to do. I am your only girl cousin."

"I'll think about it."

"Wow, Sunday. I see why Sam can't get back with you. You are hardcore."

I chuckle. "No, Sam can't get back with me because he's scum. But, I'm done thinking about forgiving you. I forgive you, girl."

"You do?"

I nod and give her a small hug. "That's how Tollivers roll."

"And you know this!" Dreya says with one hand in the air. "So now that we have that out of the way, what are you wearing to the Grammys?"

"I don't even know. Haven't had time to think about it." This I can answer honestly, because it is the truth.

"I'll have Evan send a designer to the Spelman campus. You need to look good representing Reign Records."

"No, ma'am. I don't even think so. I will go to the mall and find something. I'm not buying any thousand-dollar gowns."

Dreya laughs. "I don't pay for anything anymore! The designers want us to wear their stuff to the awards shows. As long as you remember to say their name on the red carpet. Trust me, I know how stingy you are with your money. I wouldn't even suggest it if it wasn't free."

"Oh, okay. Text me a time and date then, and it's on."

"Okay."

I pick up my backpack and sling it over my shoulder. "I've got to go and write this paper, Dreya. For real."

"Did you ever think of hiring someone to do that for you?"

I look at her like she's lost her mind. "What? My homework? No. That's called cheating."

"Oh, come on! It's just a homework assignment. You're going to take the exams, right? It's like when we used to work together on our assignments. You could just have a study buddy . . . who writes papers."

"Girl, let me get away from you before I change my mind about forgiving you."

Dreya laughs out loud. "I'm just trying to help you out!"

"You're trying to make sure I have time to work on your album."

"That too, but you are definitely stressed to the limit. I don't want to see you burn out, cuzzo."

"Let me be the one to worry about my stress level, okay? I'm straight."

"You're saying that now. But if you keep writing hit

songs, you won't need a law degree or a degree in anything for that matter. You could just live life, and live it up."

"I'm out, Dreya." I take the stairs like Sam, two at a time.

I think I'm done trying to convince everyone about my choices for my life. I want to enjoy college, and not just get a degree. I want to do music that I feel deep down in my soul. And, I want to have study dates with cute guys.

I just hope that I can have it all without losing myself in the process.

8

I just got my paper back from composition class. Another C. I slump down in my chair, totally feeling dejected.

Gia pokes me in the side. "What's wrong?"

"I got a C on my paper."

"Oh."

I watch Gia try to stealthily slip her paper in her binder without me seeing the gigantic A+ on top of it. I'm so not used to being average. I've always been stellar in everything I do, so I can't get with these middle-of-the-road grades.

Professor Due gives us yet another writing assignment based on a selection from a Toni Morrison novel called *A Mercy*. I have got to get an A on this one, for real.

After class is dismissed, Gia and I go over to meet Piper for lunch at the Manley Student Center. Mostly, we eat off campus, but this has got to be a quick lunch for me, because I have a stylist meeting me in my dorm with a boatload of clothes for the Grammys.

Piper is already here waiting for us. She smiles at us as we sit down, but I can't bring myself to match her chipperosity. I'm too bummed about my grade.

"What's wrong with you?" Piper asks.

When I don't reply, Gia says, "She got a bad grade on her paper."

"It wasn't that bad. It was a C," I say.

"Exactly," Gia says. "It wasn't that bad. Professor Due rocks, but she has high standards."

"You got an A, though. . . ."

"I got an A, because I don't have to go to the studio every other day, and I can actually do my homework. You're trying to do too much," Gia says.

"Not you too! Everyone keeps saying that to me. I can go to school and do music. It doesn't have to be one or the other."

Piper says, "Maybe you should just drop your class load some."

"No. I want to graduate with y'all. I'm not going to be here for six years trying to finish."

"Maybe, you just need to get more organized. Have you thought about hiring an assistant?" Gia asks.

"You want the job?" I ask.

"Uh, no! I am your friend, so that's not gonna work. Piper either. We're too tight. I was thinking my homeboy Kevin."

"Does he need the money or something?" I ask, unsure of how I feel about this idea, but not totally rejecting it.

"He could definitely use it. Kevin is here on full scholarship, and his grandparents are barely giving him enough to live on. If it wasn't for that on-campus meal card, he'd be starving to death, but that's not why I recommended him."

"Well, why did you say him instead of me?" Piper asks. "Because I would so make a great assistant."

"Kevin is ridiculously organized, and no boyfriend you have would ever worry about him trying to holla at you, because he would never do that."

"But Kevin is cute though," I say. "If Sam and I were still dating, he wouldn't be feeling that at all."

"You and Sam are history, right?" Piper asks. "We don't care what he would think."

Gia high-fives Piper across the table. "Okay!"

I would join in with their celebration, but I'm not ecstatic about Sam being the past, especially when I have to see him all the time. I let out a long and tired sigh.

Gia touches my arm lightly. "Don't feel bad, girl. You aren't the only one having boyfriend issues."

"You too?" My eyebrows lift in shock. Gia and Ricky are like the epitome of teenage love.

"Ricky wants to break up. He says that it's too hard staying chaste and being in a relationship." Gia sounds sad, but not angry.

"Chaste?" Piper asks. "So, you guys haven't . . . ?"

"No. We're both virgins," Gia says. "We're saving ourselves for marriage."

Piper takes a long swig of her soda. "Whoa."

"I'm a virgin too," I say.

"Are you serious?" Piper says. "Now, y'all making me feel like a skank."

I throw a French fry at her. "Pretty much."

"Whatever!" Piper says.

I turn to Gia and give her a hug, even though I'm not a hugger. She looks so sad that I make an exception.

"Are you okay?" I ask.

She nods. "I am. It's just that I'm afraid that while we're not officially together that he might find someone else."

"If he does, then he wasn't the one," Piper says. "You just have to know that."

I rub Gia's back as a few tears drop from her eyes. She doesn't go into a full-fledged cry. I don't think that's Gia's style.

"At least you have your cousin Hope on campus with him to give us the scoop," Piper says.

This makes us all burst into laughter and dries Gia's tears right up. I wish I could trust Dreya to give me the scoop on what Sam is doing in NYC. It would help me get over him if I knew Sam had moved on.

"Y'all want to help me pick out my Grammy outfit?" I ask. "It might be fun."

"Negative," Gia says. "I've got a research paper to do."

"Me either. I'm going to kick it with a guy I met when I went to sign up for a class at Morehouse."

"Is he cute?" Gia asks.

"No, girl. He's hot. He looks like a nineteen-year-old Idris Elba! He's tall, and dark, and has an incredible body."

"I'ma need you to not sound that excited!" I say. "You sound like you're about to melt into a little puddle on the floor. What's his name?"

"James, but everyone calls him L.J. He is so perfectly perfect. I'm so glad I met him. I thought I was going to stay boyfriendless."

"Maybe I need to get out more," I say, "because there seem to be hotties everywhere, and I'm totally boyfriend free."

Gia and Piper both laugh. "DeShawn would so be pouting right now if he heard you say that," Gia says.

"He's not my boyfriend, but he's definitely a hottie."

Piper says, "I heard him talking about going to the Grammys with you. He's so pumped."

"He is, isn't he? That's the effect I have on the poor boy. I hope he's able to contain his excitement."

Gia says, "Are y'all ready for our Black History Month performance? We've only got two more rehearsals. How are y'all feeling about it?"

Piper and I look at each other and then back at Gia. "You want to go first?" I ask.

"No, you," Piper says.

I clear my throat. "Gia, honey . . . I don't think I want to do this dance anymore. You told us that a lot of people would join us, but it's just the four of us. I'm not much of a dancer. I was gonna hide in the back of everybody else."

"I want to do it," Piper says, "but I think people will look at me strange, because I'm white."

"I cannot believe y'all," Gia says. "But I should've known that y'all would flake out on me."

"What about Meagan?" I ask. "Isn't she still doing it?"

"She quit after the last practice. Sent me a text message," Gia says.

I put my arm around Gia's shoulder. "I'm sorry, Gia."

She shrugs me off. "I just wish y'all had told me before. Now, I've got to look all crazy in front of our professor, because I promised this dance, and now it's not gonna happen. What happened to sisterhood, huh?"

I let out a huge sigh. "Okay, dang. I'll do it."

"Well, I'll have to change a few things if it's just going to be the two of us." Gia hugs me around my neck.

Piper groans. "Why'd you have to go there about sisterhood? I'll do it too."

Gia takes one of her arms and wraps it around Piper's neck and pulls us into a three person hug. "Yay. I knew y'all wouldn't let me down. I'm going to make us some beautiful skirts. All you need to get is a black leotard and tights."

I shake my head. How in the world did this happen? I was supposed to be getting out of this African dance thing. I just know it's going to be on YouTube, and I'm gonna be looking a straight-up mess.

"Okay then, *sisters*. I have to go and look at dresses for the Grammys," I say as I stand from the table.

"But you didn't eat anything," Piper says.

"I know. I'll get something later. That C totally ruined my appetite. Do me a favor, though. Ask L.J. if he has any friends. I think I feel like hanging out tonight."

"Did you read *A Mercy* yet?" Gia asks. "You should probably get an early start, since you've got the Grammys and everything."

"Listen here, fun police. I need a break."

Piper grins. "I'll ask him. We can go out clubbing or something. Don't hate on fun, Gia."

Gia shakes her head. "Well, whatever. I'm on scholarship, so I have to get A's. You slackers can do what you want, as long as you are in the place on Thursday, and ready to dance."

"Okay," I say. "Call me, Piper. Gia, I'll see you later."

I rush over to my dorm to meet the celebrity stylist who's going to hopefully have me looking like an A-list star for the Grammy awards. To my dismay, Dreya is standing outside my dorm with the stylist.

"Girl, I know you didn't have us waiting," Dreya says as she looks at her watch.

I ignore Dreya and extend my hand in a greeting to the stylist. "I'm sorry for the delay. I had class earlier. Sunday Tolliver, pleased to meet you."

"I am Anjelica, and I am also happy to meet you."

At first glance, Anjelica doesn't really look like someone I'd hire to dress me. She stands about four feet five inches tall, and she has shocking white hair, even though her face doesn't look older than about forty. She's wearing a blue crushed velvet cat suit, knee-high leather boots, and a leather jacket with gray fur. I sure hope she can do something other than her look, because, yeah, I'm not rocking anything that looks like that.

"Is there someone who can help carry up my samples?" Anjelica asks.

"Dreya and I can do it. There's an elevator in the dorm."

Dreya looks at me like I'm crazy. "Girl, you know I don't carry stuff. I am way too fly for that. Can't you call some of your little boyfriends?"

I let out a groan and dial DeShawn's number on my

cell phone. He answers on the first ring. "Hey, beautiful," he says.

"Hi, DeShawn." I refuse to acknowledge his greeting. "Could you do me a super huge favor?"

"Anything, but keep it PG, because I'm with Ricky and Kevin."

"Boy, stop! I'm glad you're with Ricky and Kevin though. Can y'all come over to my dorm like right now? I've got this stylist here and she's got all this stuff to haul up to my room."

"Stylist?"

"Yeah, she's gonna pick my Grammy outfit."

"Well, of course we can. We're on the Morehouse campus right now. We'll be there in like ten minutes."

"Okay. Thank you, DeShawn!" I disconnect the call and say, "They'll be here in ten minutes."

Anjelica says, "While we're waiting on them, I'm going to get some coffee. From the looks of your current ensemble, it's going to take quite a while to make you fabulous, honey."

Dreya cracks up laughing as Anjelica jumps in her Mercedes SUV and drives off.

"What are you laughing at?" I ask.

"Your non-style-having behind," Dreya says.

"Come on, let's go upstairs and wait for the guys."

When we get into my room, Dreya makes herself comfortable on my bed. "This room is too small. It's like being back at Auntie Shawn's house," she says. "When are you going to get your own spot?"

"Probably next year. Freshmen don't live off-campus really."

"You don't think they'd make an exception for you? You're a celebrity, and you need more space than this."

So, because I have a hit record and won an award I take up more space than the average person? Sometimes Dreya's logic is completely crazy, but I guess it makes sense to her.

"I've been meaning to ask you something. Did you put that video up on YouTube from Mystique's wedding?"

"No, but I wish I had!" Dreya says. "I loved how they captured Mystique's face cracking. It was the funniest!"

"That was foul, Dreya. There was nothing funny about that whole thing. How would you like someone ruining your wedding day?"

"Maybe she should've tied up all of Zac's loose ends before tying the knot."

"I think it was up to Zac to get his baby's mother in check. Why should Mystique have anything to do with that?"

Dreya shrugs. "Anyway, I don't care about her. And you need to remove yourself from the crack of her butt. She doesn't care about you. Not like Evan does. You know he's paying for the stylist out of his own pocket, because he wants you to look incredible."

"Really. This is out of the kindness of his heart? I thought it was free. I'll have to write him a thank you note."

"I'm not stupid, Sunday. I hear your sarcasm. You are tripping. Evan is your biggest fan. The clothes are free, but Anjelica is pretty expensive."

For the first time in a long time, I hear some sincerity in Dreya's voice. I think she really cares for Evan. This scares me, because the last time she put her heart out there, it was with Truth, and he was an even bigger player than Sam's trifling behind.

"I have no beef with Evan. I just don't think as highly of him as you do. I appreciate him taking care of the Grammy wardrobe. That's very generous of him."

"You better act like you know!" Dreya says.

"How long do you think this is gonna take? An hour? Two? I've got to start on this paper for my composition class."

My phone buzzes on my hip. "Hey, DeShawn. Y'all downstairs?"

"Yeah. Are we supposed to be helping the lady in the Mercedes SUV?"

"Yes, that's her. Thanks again for doing this."

"You're welcome. See you in a second."

Dreya grins at me as I disconnect the call. "What are you looking at me like that for?" she asks.

"You like him, don't you?"

"Sure. He's a cool guy and so far a good friend."

"Whatever, Sunday. You *like* him, and it's okay. It's not skanky at all to drop a loser and pick up a winner. I think it'll be good for you to kick it with someone else. Then maybe you can work with Sam without being all twisted."

"I can work with Sam just fine. As soon as he gets over the fact that we're not together anymore it'll be perfect, but he can't seem to get that through his thick skull. He keeps trying to get back together."

A knock on my door lets me know that the guys have hauled up at least one load from Anjelica's car. I swing open the door and watch in awe as they carry in box after box of shoes and several racks of dresses. By the time they're done, my room is crammed to the hilt with designer wear.

"Where do we start?" I ask, truthfully not knowing how to begin wading through the couture.

Kevin says, "I think you probably should pick a dress first. Then, you can accessorize."

Everyone stops what they're doing to stare at Kevin. "What?" he asks. "Isn't she about to select a Grammy outfit?"

"You're weird, man," DeShawn says.

"Weird maybe, but exactly right," Anjelica says.

As Anjelica whips out the first few items, the guys look for empty places to sit. Ricky takes a glance at Gia's bed and picks up one of her stuffed Tweety dolls. He holds it up to his nose, closes his eyes, and inhales. Then he gingerly places the toy back on her bed. Yeah, I don't think she has to worry about him looking for another girlfriend. Dude is totally gone over her.

Anjelica hands me three dresses. "Here, try these first."

I go into the bathroom and try the first, a burgundy velvet tube dress that has a black sparkly long sleeved vest to go with it. The fit of the dress pushes my boobs up so that they're saying hello.

This is confirmed as soon as I step out of the bathroom, by DeShawn's cheering. Kevin gives me a round of applause too.

"That is good, but it is not perfection," Anjelica says. "We can do better."

"Yeah, I don't know if I like those super dark colors on Sunday's light skin," Dreya says. "It looks kind of harsh."

I nod once and trudge back into the bathroom. The next dress is a fitted magenta silk, floor-length gown. I look in the mirror and smile. This, I like. My mother would like it too. I pin my hair into a makeshift French roll and toss on a layer of lip gloss for an extra effect.

Kevin and Ricky gasp as I come into the room this time. DeShawn says, "Okay, I change my mind. This is the one I vote for. You look incredible."

"She looks like a Disney princess, like she fixing to have a *Beauty and the Beast* birthday party or something," Dreya says. "I dislike."

Anjelica says, "I disagree with you. I picked this out specifically for Sunday. It has an understated, sweet and innocent sexiness. You would never be able to pull it off. On you, the innocence would look contrived, but on Sunday, it is perfection."

Dreya rolls her eyes. "If I wanted to do innocent, I could. I like being a bad girl."

"Naiveté is not something you can fake, my dear."

"Well, whatever. I liked the other outfit better," Dreya says.

Kevin says, "You've been outvoted."

We all watch as Anjelica moves through the boxes, cases, and containers with the ease of a master chef in her very own kitchen. She pulls out the perfect pair of silver, crystal-encrusted shoes.

"Try these."

They are exactly my size. I gotta give it to Evan, Anjelica is good!

"Is Gia going to be back soon?" Ricky asks.

"I'm not sure," I say. "I think she's gonna be gone for a while. She's doing some research."

"Maybe I better just go now, then. I don't want to risk seeing her. Kev and DeShawn, can y'all carry the stuff back down without me?"

"Yeah," Kevin says. "We got it. But are you sure you don't want to see Gi-Gi?"

"I'm not sure I should, plus I'm not one-hundred-percent sure she's even talking to me." There is such melancholy in Ricky's voice that I want to jump up and give him a hug.

"All right then, bro, I'll see you back on campus later," DeShawn says.

"Bye, Ricky!" I say. "I know you don't want to see Gia right now, but I think she might like a text later if you think about it."

Ricky gives me a bittersweet smile. "Okay, I'll do that."

After he leaves, Dreya bursts into laughter. "Y'all have the most ridiculous situations. Don't tell me. They broke up because they would be better as friends."

"Wrong," Kevin says. "And you're not about to sit here and clown my two best friends, so can you change the subject back to Sunday's accessories?"

Dreya's jaw drops. "Did this lame just try to check me? Boy, do you know who you're talking to?"

"Yep. Dreya Tolliver, cousin of one of my favorite singers, Sunday Tolliver, although I'm waiting to see what she does on her follow-up record to solidify my fan status."

Everyone, except Dreya, cracks up laughing. I haven't

heard anyone call her Dreya outside of family, ever since she released her first record.

"You better get your friends, Sunday," Dreya warns. But now, we're laughing so hard that she's not threatening to anyone.

I hop over to Kevin in my dress and pat him on the back. "Dude. You are so hired."

"I am? For what?"

"Gia suggested that I hire you as an assistant, and I would love to have you. Anybody who stands up to Evilene over there is the perfect choice for me."

"Score!" Kevin jumps into the air and pumps his fist.

"You've got to be kidding me!" Dreya says. "Now I've got to see this dude on a regular basis?"

Kevin smiles at Dreya. "You shouldn't be so hasty. You might just like me if you tried me out."

DeShawn gives him a fist bump and I almost collapse from laughter. Dreya's face turns a crimson shade of red and she balls up her fists at her side.

"I already have a man, thank you. A real man. A real, rich man. Your broke self can step, for real."

Kevin shrugs. "You had your chance. Don't come back later trying to holler."

This is the straw that breaks the camel's back for Dreya. She hops up from my bed and storms out of my room. If she hadn't slammed the door behind her, she would've heard our giggles all the way down the hall.

"Kevin, don't make an enemy of Dreya," I say. "She can be so annoying when she's trying to get revenge."

"Ah, I'm just messing with her. I'm actually a huge fan.

I just don't want her to think she can walk all over me, because that's not about to happen."

"Well, if she ain't know before, she knows now!" De-Shawn says. "You put her in check." He emphasizes his point by making a little check mark with his index finger.

"Here, darling. Put on this diamond choker, and see what it looks like with the dress," Anjelica says.

I struggle with the clasp for a moment, until DeShawn jumps up and says, "Let me."

I feel his hot breath on my neck as he slowly clamps the choker. It doesn't take this long to put on a piece of jewelry, so I know he's taking his time on purpose. When he sits back down, Anjelica squeals at her creation and holds up a mirror for me to see.

"Once we get you in hair and makeup, you are going to be a goddess, honey. Ms. Drama might be mad she and Evan sent me over here."

"How am I gonna get this stuff to Los Angeles?" I ask. "I don't like to check bags."

Anjelica tosses her head back and giggles. "You are a celebrity, honey! You're going to have to check a bag. But not this time. I will be in L.A. with everything you need because I'm dressing all of the Reign Records crew."

"Can you bring a tuxedo for my date?" I ask. I point at DeShawn and he grins.

Anjelica says, "Of course. What about your assistant? Will he be attending also?"

"You want to come, Kevin? I will probably need you."

His eyes widen. "Absolutely. I might have to turn in some assignments in advance, but I am so down for this."

Kevin and DeShawn help Anjelica pack up all of her boxes and racks, and they make several trips to take them back downstairs. There's nothing like having strong boys when you need them!

When they're done, the boys come back upstairs and sprawl out on my floor.

"Hey, y'all can't stay long. I have some reading to do and a paper to start!" I make my declaration, but I'm not sure if I really mean it. I am not in the mood for reading.

"We'll be quiet. We just want to hang out in the Grammy award winner's room."

"I haven't won yet, don't jinx it," I say.

Kevin frowns. "You can't jinx a blessing. What God has for you is for you."

"As churchy as Kevin is, I agree with him," DeShawn says. "You are blessed, and you deserve the best, so I'm glad you decided to do yourself a favor and ask me out on a date."

"It's not a real date, DeShawn."

"Yes, it is. But next time we go out, I'm paying."

Kevin laughs, "But you're broke."

"What does Sunday need with a rich dude? She's already paid. She needs a guy who's gonna keep it real, and not play her. Am I right?"

I feel that no matter how I answer this question it'll be a trap. DeShawn is growing on me, no doubt about that. A girl can only take but so much of a hot guy before he starts to wear her down. But, I know that I'm still wounded, and those hurts are so fresh that they're sore to the touch.

"You're right. That's exactly what I need, DeShawn, but I'm afraid your timing is really bad."

"Nah, my timing's fine. I know you're not ready now, but when the time is right, we'll get together. It's bound to happen."

"Come on, Romeo," Kevin says. "Let's go, so Sunday can do her homework."

Kevin and DeShawn get up to go, and when they're almost out the door, DeShawn steps back inside and kisses my cheek.

When I snatch away from him, he says, "Sorry. I've wanted to do that this entire afternoon. I won't do it again. I promise."

I narrow my eyes at him as that gleeful smile plays across his lips. His promise sounds suspect to me. Very suspect.

Finally the boys are gone and I'm alone with my thoughts. I take out my book and spread out on my bed. I try to read, but my mind keeps drifting off. Thinking about DeShawn.

Then, for some reason, I wonder about Gia and Ricky. They have the kind of relationship I want. The kind of friendship that says, *I'd rather be apart than hurt you.* Is that too much to ask?

9

Bethany just sang an incredible set at the House of Blues in Atlanta in preparation for album release. The crowd gave her a standing ovation and called her back for not one but two encores. I think she could've kept going another few hours without stopping.

Now I'm standing in the hallway outside her dressing room. I raise my hand to knock, but then I change my mind and lower it again. I'm torn about being too friendly toward Bethany. I'd like to offer my congratulations on her performance, but I don't want her to think that means we're best friends again. She messed that up our senior year of high school when she dated my ex-boyfriend, and then hooked up with my cousin's then-boyfriend, Truth.

While I'm deciding whether or not to enter, Big D walks up with a huge smile on his face. "That girl can blow, right? After this record drops, it's a wrap. We're talking multiple Grammys and MTV video awards."

"That's what's up," I say. "Are you going in to talk to Bethany?"

"Yeah. You too?"

I shrug. "Hadn't decided yet."

"Come on." Big D takes my wrist in his hand as he knocks on the door. I hear Bethany croak "Come in" with a tiny, scratchy voice.

Big D opens the door, and a gigantic cloud of smoke billows out of the small dressing room. From the glassy look in Bethany's eyes, the smoke isn't from your average cigarette either. She's doing Sam's favorite illegal substance—marijuana.

I shake my head, the smell of the room bothering me. "I should go. Good show."

"Wait, don't leave." Bethany reaches out and grips my hand as if for dear life.

"Okay . . ."

Big D kisses Bethany on the top of her head. She smiles so brightly that you'd think he was some kind of teen heartthrob. "You did good, Ms. Whooty," Big D says.

Ms. Whooty is Big D's nickname for Bethany. The white girl with a big booty = whooty. My little cousin Manny coined it first, and then after that it stuck.

"Thanks, Big D. Y'all don't know how much it means to me that y'all are here. My mama didn't show up. My sisters neither. But I guarantee you they'll be the first ones with they hands out when the money comes."

"You don't need me to tell you that you can sing, but I love the way you sing my music. You might want to lay off the weed, though. Coat your throat with poison enough times, and you might not have a voice anymore."

Bethany waves one hand in the air. "Oh, this? This ain't an everyday thing, Sunday. This is just for after my shows. I get so wired being out there on stage. The whole show is like one big stimulant. I was just trying to come back down again."

I don't reply to her reasoning. She sounds like a drug addict with her excuses and explanations. All I know is that she's smoking weed out in the open as if there's nothing wrong with it—and I'm not with that.

"Well, I don't want that poison clogging up my lungs. I'm going outside. Good job, again, on the show."

Instead of waiting for Big D to come out of the dressing room, I go back out into the restaurant to enjoy the live jazz musician who is serenading the customers while they eat dinner. I take a seat at the bar, order a virgin daiquiri, and relax. My phone buzzes with a text message from Sam.

Thinkin' about you and missing you. Wish you would call.

I sigh at the sentimental words. He thinks I'm just supposed to immediately forgive him because he's decided that he wants me back? Sam's flimsy explanations of his dirt don't exactly count as apologies, so I can't even say that he's given me an honest apology.

"Are you Sunday Tolliver?" A guy about my age has slid onto the barstool next to me.

"Yes, I am."

The guy lets out a shrill scream. "I cannot believe this! I was just saying the other day that I was gonna carry my demo around in my pocket until I meet you. And here you are just two days later."

"Your demo?"

"Yes! I am Montray, a singer-slash-actor-slash-song-writer, but not necessarily in that order. Could you hook a brotha up and listen to my demo?"

My eyes dart around the room, looking for anyone to save me, or at the very least an escape route. When neither are readily available, I give Montray my friendliest smile.

"I can listen, but um . . . I can't really give you a record deal. I'm just an artist myself."

Montray's eyebrows dip so deeply that they appear to be one giant brow. "So that's how you are, huh? You got yours, but you can't reach back and help somebody else?"

"I . . . uh . . ."

"That's how it's goin' down?" Montray's loud voice is drawing attention our way.

"Look, I don't want any trouble. I said I would listen to your demo, so chill, okay?"

Montray stands from his bar stool, and I realize how tall and wide he is. Where in the world is Big D when I need him?

"Yeah, you gonna listen to my demo, right now. Let's go. I know you got a CD player in your car."

"I'm not going outside with you."

Montray grabs my arm and yanks me from the stool. "Yes, you are. I'm trying to get this record deal money, ya heard?"

Hot tears sting my eyes as I try to free myself from Montray's grasp. Then, someone taps Montray on the shoulder. It's Sam!

"Playa, I'm gonna need you to take your hands off of her," Sam says in a strong and forceful voice.

"Man, back up off me!"

When Montray doesn't comply with Sam's request, Sam does what I've seen him do before. He drops Montray to the floor with a two-punch combination that probably has the wannabe celebrity seeing stars.

I exhale a breath of relief. As much as Sam gets on my nerves, I have never been happier to see him.

"What are you doing here?" I ask as Sam pulls me away from the bar and toward the club's exit door.

"Shouldn't you be saying, 'Thank you, Sam, for saving me'?"

I unravel my hand from his. "Thank you. I'm so glad that you're here."

"That's more like it. I came to see Bethany's show, but my flight got delayed, so I didn't make it in time."

"Oh, well, she did a good job. Big D thinks she's going to go at least gold in the first week of her release if her single does well."

"Mo money, mo money, mo money!" Sam's monotone voice doesn't match his words.

"You sound real excited about that."

Sam clears his throat and smiles. "Well, if I gain more money than I can spend, but I don't have my lady by my side, what good is it?"

I roll my eyes and walk through the open door. "It'll be a lot of money whether I'm by your side or not."

"Where's your car?" Sam asks.

"I valet parked."

"Give me your ticket."

I almost refuse, because I don't want Sam to do boyfriend-type things anymore. I don't want him walking me to my car, tipping the valet for me, or anything else. I just want him to be my record producer.

"I need to tell Big D I'm out of here," I say, remembering that I left Big D in Bethany's dressing room.

Sam shakes his head. "Call him from the road, or even when you're back safe at your dorm. As a matter of fact, I'm following you back."

"That is not necessary."

"Yes, it is! Sunday, you just had some random dude put his hands on you." Sam hands the valet my ticket.

"Okay, okay. Follow me back, but you're not walking me in."

Sam lifts his eyebrow. "Listen, I know you don't want to get back together. I understand. But I am walking you to the door. And I'm going to have Big D hire a bodyguard for you."

"I'm not walking around with a bodyguard. That's so . . . so . . . Mystique."

"At least when you go out kicking it. You've got to be safe."

"Maybe when I go out, but only then. I'm not walking around campus with a bodyguard."

"You could always hire me," Sam says with a smile.

"You're no bodyguard, Sam. Plus, you live in New York. And uh, I don't really like you that much, remember?"

Sam chuckles. "I've beat up two guys for you. I'd move back to Atlanta to take care of you. And I am convinced that your not liking me is a temporary condition. One day you'll learn the truth, and you'll be sad you kicked me to the curb."

"You're not moving back to Atlanta."

The valet driver pulls my car up and Sam laughs out loud. "When are you buying a new car, Sunday?"

"When this one breaks. I'm not into cars all like that."

Sam hands the valet his ticket. "Can you bring mine around too? I'm going to follow Ms. Tolliver home."

Sam opens my car door for me and I get inside. "You are just super polite, Sam. I'd almost mistake you for a really great guy if I didn't know the truth."

"Sunday, haven't you ever heard of forgiveness?"

What? The nerve of him! It always seems like the people who want to lecture you on forgiveness are the ones always doing wrong stuff to you. He's not going to get over like that.

"I have heard of it. I've used it a few times when it's come to you as well. I don't have to keep putting up with your crap, Sam. Maybe you'll know how to treat your next girlfriend."

"I'm hoping you're going to be my next girlfriend."

"Take the N and the T off of next and then you'll have it right."

The valet pulls up in Sam's rental car. "Sunday, I'm right behind you."

I don't wait for Sam to get settled into his ride. I peel off and let him smell the burning rubber from my tires. He can walk me to my dorm—but he'll have to catch me first.

And I drive fast.

10

I must really, really love Gia, because she's got me standing before about two hundred of my Spelman sisters and some administrators, barefoot in a bright yellow and orange skirt with a head wrap to match. Piper's outfit is identical except her colors are green and yellow. Gia, who stands front and center in our little dance triangle, is wearing red and yellow.

Nervous cannot even begin to describe how I feel. You'd think I'd be used to getting in front of people and performing, and I am, but this time there's no mic in my hand. When I do a show, if I goof up the choreography, it's okay, because I can just start singing extra hard, like I wasn't supposed to dance on that part anyway. This is totally different.

I give a quick side glance to Piper, who appears to be confident, but her skin is flushed and red, telling me that maybe she's a little bit nervous too. Gia on the other hand has a look of intensity on her face.

The only time I see her concentration crack is when DeShawn, Ricky, and Kevin walk in and sit in the back row of the auditorium. Gia bites her lip and then smiles.

Just as I feel myself begin to relax, the music blares through the speakers. The African drum beats and the xylophone's chime take me back to Gia's brutal rehearsals. It's as if I can hear her voice in my head counting out the beats.

And then we start to move! Every shoulder bounce and deep bend is on point. Every turn, spin, and jump is executed dang near perfectly. I get off for a half second, but I don't think anyone can tell but me.

Then, almost as quickly as it started, the song is over. We link arms and take a deep bow as everyone in the room applauds. Some people even stand, but no one is cheering louder than our own personal boy fan club in the back of the room.

Our performance was the finale to the program and Dr. Brooks, our professor for the African Diaspora class closes it out as soon as we leave the stage. My heart is racing still, I guess from the adrenaline rush I got right before we started.

Everyone congratulates us as they leave the auditorium. I smile and take the background, and let Gia have this moment. She worked really hard on this and she deserves the congrats and the extra credit.

Ricky walks up to her holding a bouquet of flowers and a Tweety balloon. He hugs her and hands her the flowers. "You were awesome, Gi-Gi!"

"I didn't think you would come," Gia says as she accepts the flowers.

"Why did you think that? I wouldn't miss anything like this," Ricky says.

Kevin says, "Before you two start getting all sentimental, I just want to say that your choreography was flawless, Gia. Are you sure you want to be a computer programmer? You looked like an Alvin Ailey dancer up there."

"I love dancing, but my mom told me that I should pick something practical to study," Gia says. "Programming computers will pay the bills. Know what I mean?"

"But you should do what you love," Piper says. "That's the only way to be happy."

Gia turns to me. "Can you back me up here? You love music, but you're getting a law degree. We can do both, right? We can have what we love and still get a paycheck."

Before I can answer, DeShawn says, "Or you could get the paycheck doing what you love."

I shake my head and laugh. "This is an endless debate that no one ever wins."

DeShawn runs his hand down my right arm and then squeezes my hand. The intimacy of his gesture makes me want to pull away, but for some reason I don't.

He says, "You were great up there too, Sunday. What can't you do?"

"Apparently, get an A in my composition class."

Piper laughs out loud. "You can too get an A. Stop saying that. I've got to go, y'all. I have a date with my Morehouse man."

"You sound like Meagan," I say.

"There is something to be said for my Morehouse brothers," Kevin says. "We are an elite bunch."

DeShawn rolls his eyes. "Ricky, let's drop off Mr. Elite and go grab something to eat."

"Okay," Ricky replies. "Gia . . . are you hungry? Want to go with us?"

"Only if Sunday comes too." The pleading look in her eyes convinces me of my response, even though I need to study.

"All right, but I can't stay out late. I have to finish my selection from *A Mercy.*"

"You're not done with that yet?" Gia asks. "You are the biggest procrastinator."

"I know, right? Let's go change out of our leotards so we can eat."

Gia says, "Okay, Ricky give us like fifteen minutes and we'll meet you out front."

About a half hour later, we're crammed into a booth at the Busy Bee Café, and scanning the menu for our dinner choices.

"I'm getting fried chicken, macaroni and cheese, and greens," I say as I slam the menu shut.

Gia laughs. "You get the same thing every time, so why do you even need the menu?"

"Sometimes I get the smothered pork chops or different side dishes. I just have to know what I'm in the mood for, and right now it is fried chicken!"

"Since you did such a good job, you should treat yourself," Ricky says.

"Dr. Brooks personally thanked me for stepping up to the plate," Gia says. "I'm so glad we decided to do it."

I laugh out loud. "I don't know if I really decided to do anything. You guilt tripped me and Piper until we had no other choice."

"Too bad she couldn't hang out with us tonight," De-Shawn says. "Piper is cool."

"Yes, she is, but she is totally gone over this L.J. dude," Gia says. "I was listening to her on the phone with him the other day and she is completely sickening."

DeShawn and I make eye contact and laugh. Up until recently Ricky and Gia were equally sickening, so Gia's observation of Piper's romance is pretty funny.

"What?" Gia asks. "Oh, I know what y'all are trying to say, but Ricky and I had been dating for a long time. She just met this dude."

"I didn't say anything," I say. "Meagan is lost to us too, I think. She hasn't even been around. Piper says she's hardly ever on campus, except for class, and when she is in the dorm, it's always when Piper is out with L.J. They barely see each other anymore."

"We may have lost one of our sisters to boy craziness," Gia says.

"And another is following quickly behind."

DeShawn laughs. "So, I guess it's just y'all against the dating world, huh?"

"Pretty much," Gia says. She is genuinely somber, but I'm on the verge of cracking up. DeShawn is clearly teasing us, but Gia's not taking it that way.

"Come on. Let's go up through the line and get our food, before I perish," I say.

Ricky laughs. "Perish? You sound like Kevin now. You two have been hanging out too much."

"We haven't been hanging out, we've been working. Kevin is the assistant of my dreams. He's printed up a complete itinerary for me for Grammys weekend. He hired a car service to take us to the airport and another to pick us up when we land in L.A. He's a total dream."

"I told you he would be," Gia says. "And you were ready to hire Piper's boy-crazy behind."

"I was. Thank you for convincing me otherwise."

As we walk up to the line, I watch Gia and Ricky brush against one another although they are really trying to pretend that it's not on purpose. I keep catching them stealing glances at each other when they think no one is looking. They are totally pitiful and I feel sorry for their pain.

I don't care how much Gia tries to fight it, she's boy crazy too. It seems like I'm the only one who's been unlucky in love. But, I guess there's something to be said for solitude.

When I figure out what it is, I'll let you know.

11

"Who are you wearing?" The extra perky red-carpet reporter smiles at me and shoves the microphone in my face. This is only the second time I've done this, and I'm not at all used to the flashing light-bulbs and rapid-fire questions coming my direction like bullets.

I blink a few times, as if I didn't hear the question. It's crazy, I'm on the red carpet at the Grammys and all I can think about is the paper that I didn't finish writing for my composition class. I blink a few times and reply. "The dress is vintage Versace and the shoes are Jimmy Choo."

I've coupled my pretty-in-magenta gown with a roller set pinned to the one side and cascading over my shoulder. DeShawn is incredibly dapper. I was clutching to his arm for dear life until he gently slipped his arm around my waist to move me down the red carpet.

"Well, you look fabulous!"

And just like that, the reporter is attacking another celebrity. DeShawn says, "Why didn't she ask me who I'm wearing?"

"Maybe she didn't recognize you."

DeShawn chuckles, "Well, she better Google me or something, 'cause I'm somebody too."

"Yes, you are," I say. "Tonight, I'm glad you're here with me."

Right behind us on the red carpet is the rest of the Reign Records posse. Sam has his arm around his mother, who looks pleased as punch to be on the red carpet. We briefly make eye contact as I turn and watch them talk to the reporters. I look away first when I see the sadness in his eyes.

I stop in front of another smiling reporter. "Are you excited about your Song of the Year and Best New Artist nominations? Do you think you'll win?"

I chuckle. "I am very honored to be nominated, and I certainly hope that I win."

"And you're performing tonight too?" the reporter asks. "You've had quite a busy year haven't you?"

"Yes, I'm singing my current single, and it has been ridiculously busy for me, but I'm excited. I love the thrill of it all."

"Even competing against your cousin for the Best New Artist crown?" The reporter smiles from ear to ear, so I grin right back.

"Of course. She deserves it as much as I do. Drama is an amazing singer. We've sung together our entire lives."

DeShawn nudges me forward when Sam and the rest of the Reign Records artists are basically on our heels, but not before I see the angry glares exchanged between Sam and DeShawn. Boys having testosterone battles.

Finally we're inside, and the seating arrangement is crazy. DeShawn is on one side of me and my songwriting partner ex-boyfriend is on the other side. I don't know if this is someone's idea of a joke, but I'm not laughing.

"You want me to move?" Sam asks when he sees the little sign with his name on it.

"No. I'm straight. They probably did it because we're nominated for an award together. It's all good."

"What about your boyfriend?" Sam asks. "You okay with that dude?"

I quickly reply, "My date does not care who I sit next to. He knows that I'm here with him."

I'm not so sure that DeShawn's response would've been the same as mine. But I can't let him get into an argument with Sam at the Grammys. That would be all bad. He'd end up on every blog on the Internet in the morning.

Dreya and Evan have, I guess, decided to let the world know about their romance. The two of them are completely embarrassing. I don't think the second row at the Grammys is the place to make out. I know the show hasn't started yet, but my insides cringe with each slurping sound.

Big D, Shelly, Dilly, and Bethany are seated a row behind us, and there are chairs marked for Mystique and Zac in the front row. The only one missing from Big D's original crew is rapper Truth. According to the bloggers, since he was not nominated for any Grammys, nor was he asked to perform, he was staging his own personal boycott of the show. I'm not sure if anyone even cares.

Mystique's entrance into the auditorium is an event in and of itself. She's wearing a fitted silver gown that glimmers and clings in all the right places. Zac is debonair in his tuxedo, but he has on sunglasses inside. It really annoys me when people do that.

"Mystique looks incredible," DeShawn whispers. "If she wasn't with Zac, I would so try to holler at her."

"What! I thought you were trying to get with me!"

DeShawn laughs out loud. "So, when I tell you I want to get with you, the answer is no, but you're still jealous of another chick? How's that work?"

"That's how girls are," I say. "We're pretty selfish."

"I'll tell you a secret. Guys are pretty selfish too. I think we might be worse than y'all."

Sam grunts under his breath. I wonder if he wants to contribute anything to my conversation with DeShawn. I'm sure he could shed lots of light on guys being selfish. Outside of Dreya, Sam has to be the most selfish person I know.

I lean forward and look down the aisle to get Dreya's attention when she comes up for air from Evan's vacuum lips. When she finally looks up, I mouth the words, *Good luck*. She smiles and winks at me, but doesn't wish it back. I know Dreya, so this is good enough. She doesn't really want me to win the Best New Artist Award, but I think she'll be okay with it if I do.

Mystique turns around and smiles, "You look gorgeous, Sunday. Where did you get that vintage Versace dress?"

"Evan sent a stylist for me."

She lifts an eyebrow and bites her heavily lipsticked lips. "He did?"

"Yeah. I think she was from New York."

"He's pulling out all the stops, huh? Good luck on your categories."

"Good luck to you also." Mystique is nominated for Best R & B Performance and Album of the Year. She's expected to win them both, since the competition this year is not really that strong. Mystique pats Sam on the knee affectionately before she turns back around in her seat.

Over the next hour, we watch everyone who's anyone in the music industry walk in and take seats. The positions of the seats let you know how relevant each person is in the industry right now. With the front-and-center seating of the Reign Records crew, I guess we're some of the most important in the building—not bad for a bunch of kids from Lithonia.

About a third of the way through the show, they announce the Best New Artist award. In fact, I'm backstage preparing for my performance when they announce the winner, a country artist named Shay Graham. I didn't realize that I was holding my breath until I exhale. I also realize how much I wanted to win. I blink back a tear as I watch Shay accept her award from backstage.

My reaction to losing is nothing like Dreya's. She had stood from her seat as if she was anticipating them calling her name. The camera captures her shocked and angry reaction, her mouthing the word *What?*, and Evan pulling her back down to her seat. The whole exchange is only a few seconds long, but etched into history.

I have no choice but to shake off my disappointment, because it's time for me to sing. Prior to the show, Big D and Evan tried to convince me to use a vocal track, just in case anything went wrong with the performance, but I was totally against it. I want every performance to be one-hundred-percent me singing. If I ever get to the point where my voice doesn't sound good on stage, I'm throwing in the towel. I refuse to be a studio creation.

Dilly and Bethany introduce me for the performance. It makes me laugh that the two of them have to have fake, jokey banter on stage when they are exes. At least they have a better relationship than me and Sam.

Once I'm on stage in my fitted blue minidress, I sing my heart out. "The Highlight" is probably my favorite song off the record, but I've added some extra embellishments for this show. I have the band stop playing on the last note, so that I can hit it a cappella. The note is so high and so clear that when I stop singing there is a huge pause, as if everyone in the room has sucked in their breath. But after the pause, the applause is incredibly and thunderously loud.

Everyone is clapping, but for some reason, I focus in on Sam, who is on his feet clapping and whistling like he doesn't have any sense. DeShawn is standing too, but Sam's reaction is straight-up foolish.

I don't start calming down until I'm back in my seat and next to DeShawn. He gives me a one-armed hug when I sit, and Big D pats me on my back.

"Great job," Big D says.

DeShawn whispers, "You were incredible."

Sam says nothing, but I do catch him glancing at me a

couple of times out of the corner of his eye. It's a shame that we've deteriorated to the point where he can't even tell me that he liked my performance.

They get to the Song of the Year award, and I don't even feel myself get nervous again. I don't expect to win in this category—I never did. There are too many song-writing veterans in the mix this year. My best chance of winning my first Grammy was in the Best New Artist category. I'm so relaxed that my shoes are kicked off in front of me. I get my hands ready to clap for whoever the winner will be.

Then, KeKe Palmer and Justin Bieber say, "And the winner is 'Can U See Me.' "

Oh my goodness! Am I in the cotton-picking Twilight Zone or something? I jump up from my seat, and Sam starts pulling me to the stage, but then I realize I'm not wearing shoes! I snatch away from Sam and run back to my seat to put my shoes on. Everyone in the crowd seems to think this is funny, and even though I'm super embarrassed, I have to laugh too.

Sam waits for me to get on stage before he starts saying his thank-yous, so I dash up the stairs holding up my dress like I'm Cinderella racing back home before the clock strikes midnight.

When I get up to the podium, I pick up the Grammy and look at it. Then I look at the audience and say, "For real? Song of the year? I so didn't expect this award, so y'all know I don't have a speech prepared. I do know that I need to thank God, my mama, and everybody in the Reign Records crew, Evan, Big D, Drama, Dilly, and Bethany. All of y'all. I want to thank all of my friends at

Spelman for keeping me grounded. Of course, I can't forget my mentor, Mystique. And I have the best songwriting partner on the planet!"

I move out of the way and let Sam step to the microphone. "Um, I'm shocked at this award too, but Grammy committee, thank you very much. I'd like to thank my mother, and um . . . I want to thank you, Sunday. You are my muse."

Except for the rapid blinking of my eyes, my body is frozen in place with shock. Is he serious with this? I'm his muse? He is so being Captain Uncomfortable right now, because I don't even know how I should react to this.

So, I give him a half smile and rush off the stage, holding the Grammy. I hear Sam's steps behind me, and I hear him whispering my name, but I don't want to stop. But of course, I have to stop and do the press room interviews that you do after winning an award. This halts my escape from Sam and his unchecked, embarrassing emotions.

"Sunday's your muse?" I could choke this reporter right now. Why would that be the first question she asked?

Sam smiles and nods. "She is. Before I met her, my songs were just okay, but the day she walked into our studio and told Truth his song wasn't tight, I was taken by her. We've created some beautiful music together."

"How do you feel about that, Sunday? Is Sam your muse too?"

Grrr! I clench and unclench my fists at my sides and give her the fakest smile ever. "Sam is the best songwriting partner I could've dreamed of having. He totally rocks."

"What's next for the two of you? Any projects in the works?"

Sam says, "We've got several Reign Records projects. Bethany's album drops in the spring, and we're currently in the studio with Drama on her sophomore release. Then, we'll get to work on another Sunday Tolliver album."

"Wow, that's a lot," the reporter says. "How in the world do you have time for school work?"

"It's challenging," I say. "Right now I have a paper I need to write by Tuesday, so ask me when I get my grades if I'm handling it well."

"I'm sure you'll be fine," the reporter says. She nods to the cameraman, signaling that she's done.

When I see Sam opening his mouth to say something to me, I make a mad dash toward the exit. I need to get back over to DeShawn before Sam tries to declare his love for me again. I'm not trying to hear that tonight.

"You aren't even gonna congratulate me?" Sam asks.

I stop and turn toward Sam. His jaw hangs open, giving him a surprised look. "Congratulations."

"You said that like you meant it," Sam replies sarcastically.

"What do you want me to do, Sam? Jump up and down and give you a hug? It's not going down like that."

I spin on one very high and pointy heel, and this time I make it to the exit with no further interruptions. I don't know if Sam is in shock or if he's given up, but it doesn't matter which, as long as he leaves me alone with my thoughts.

I emerge from the press room to another backstage area. Mystique is back here—waiting to present an award with Zac. She holds out both arms and squeezes her hands in a hugging gesture. I walk into her embrace and return it with one of my own.

"You should've gotten Best New Artist too, but I think they frown upon giving multiple Grammy wins to someone so freshly in the business. It's almost like someone doesn't think you've finished paying your dues." Mystique says this in such a nonchalant manner that you'd think she just said, "I made you some grilled cheese."

"It's all right. I'll take the one win! I'm thrilled about it, dues or no dues."

Zac smiles and hugs me too. "You and Sam are brilliant. It was only a matter of time before someone recognized it."

"I saw it from day one!" Mystique says. "They're going to be in the business for a long time, Zac, probably even after we retire."

"I'm never retiring. I'll be a hundred years old, wearing some jeans and sneakers and holding a mic in my hand. And I'll take out every emcee in my path, just like I was twenty-five years old." Zac throws his head back and cackles at his own comment, like the very thought of his retirement tickles him.

Mystique shakes her head. "Anyway. Congratulations, girl. Are you going to the Epsilon Records after-party?"

I nod my head. "Of course."

"Good. Then, we'll toast your success later on."

Unfortunately, I've been made to feel that the Epsilon Records after-Grammy party is mandatory, and that I really don't have any other choice but to attend. I'd much rather be back on campus finishing my paper!

Zac says, "You and Sam looked good together on stage. You need to go ahead and drop that lame and get back with my homeboy."

"DeShawn is not a lame."

"Dude is a male video vixen. Do you see any rappers bringing the chicks from their videos on the red carpet? That's not a good look for you, Sunday. Step your game up."

And by stepping my game up does he mean that I should ham it up on the red carpet with my cheating, weed smoking ex-boyfriend? That's a good look?

"DeShawn is cool people, but I expect you to defend your homeboy," I say. "Maybe next time you'll pull his collar before he cheats on his girlfriend."

"Sam's his own man."

And obviously, I'm my own woman. At some point, these men trying to run my life are going to recognize it.

"See y'all at the party!" I say with a dismissive wave of my hand.

12

The Epsilon Records Grammy after-party is crunk as what! So crunk that I stop wishing I was back at the dorm doing homework as soon as I step inside. They really pulled out all the stops on this one. It makes their American Music Awards party look like a straight-up fail.

"Dance with me!" Dreya squeals as she pulls me away from DeShawn. She's in a good mood, and clearly that mood is induced by whatever alcoholic beverage she has in her hand.

I follow Dreya to the middle of the packed dance floor. The song playing is a rock track off of one of Epsilon's Grammy winners. Dreya closes her eyes and sways to the music, and I do the same except I keep my eyes open and scan the room.

Everyone from the Reign Records crew is in the house. It looks like DeShawn and I were the last to arrive, but I stayed after the show and signed autographs outside the

Shrine Auditorium with Mystique. She said that loyal fans were made by doing things like that and not by showing up at parties.

I check out Big D and Shelly as they sit at a booth in the corner. Big D looks uncomfortable squeezing his massive belly into the small space, but Shelly looks downright evil. Her arms are folded across her chest and her lips are poked out.

"What's wrong with Shelly?" I ask Dreya over the loud, bumping music.

"I don't know," Dreya says in a slur. "Big D prolly did what he always does—holla at some random chick. Shelly's stupid for staying with him."

"I have no idea why she puts up with him."

Dreya laughs. "Really, you have no idea. Girl, bye. It's about the dollar bills."

"I guess you would know, huh."

"I ain't even in that category, playa. Evan is fine, he's rich, and he works out."

Dreya takes another swig off her beverage, closes her eyes again, and goes back to dancing. She looks like she's having a good time, but I wonder how many girls Evan has hit on this evening.

The song finishes and another one starts, this time one of Zac the Zillionaire's cuts. Since Dreya's eyes are still closed as she drops down low and sweeps the floor with her behind, I leave her to her dancing.

I narrow my eyes and look around the room at the small clusters of people next to the bar, and then at the larger groups seated at and on tables. Finally, I see who I'm looking for—DeShawn.

He's holding up the wall and gazing in my direction. When he sees me looking at him he smiles and waves. He's still wearing his tuxedo, but he's taken off his bow tie, and has unbuttoned the top three buttons of his shirt. He looks like the cover of a magazine, but then he always does. He's perfect. Too perfect. But tonight, he's all that I'm working with. I start to walk toward him, but he rushes to meet me.

"You a'ight?" DeShawn asks as he leads me to the dance floor.

I nod. "Dreya is intoxicated. She was getting on my nerves."

"No one told her that underage drinking is bad?"

I laugh. "No, DeShawn. She was absent that day of school. Or maybe she was cutting class."

"At least she isn't driving."

"You sure know how to look on the bright side, De-Shawn. I soooo love that about you."

He takes one of my hands and spins me around. "Dance with me, Sunday! Stop being so serious."

"Can we go?" I ask DeShawn.

"Yeah, but where are we going?"

I shrug. "Let's catch a cab to Roscoe's and get some chicken and waffles. I'm so over this."

"You want to tell anyone we're leaving?" DeShawn asks.

I shake my head. "No. I'm grown. I don't answer to any of them."

DeShawn bites his lip in thought. "I think it would be better if we mention it to someone. Big D, maybe? Just in case something happens. . . ."

"Tell whoever you want. I'll be by the door and ready to go."

I storm off the dance floor and for a split second I think of leaving DeShawn too. I don't want to tell Big D anything.

Right before my escape, DeShawn jogs back over to me. "Okay, girl, let's go get our grub on."

I say nothing as I let DeShawn open the door to the club, and talk to a limo driver out front.

"I said let's get a cab," I fuss.

DeShawn says, "This is easier and free."

"Yeah, and as soon as we pull up, the paparazzi are gonna start snapping pictures. Let's be a little bit more low key than that."

DeShawn sighs, and talks to the limo driver again. Then he turns back to me and says, "The limo driver says that the paparazzi are out tonight anyway because of the Grammys. He says you don't want to get snapped stepping out of a cab."

I shake my head and climb into the limo, since apparently DeShawn is gonna run this into the ground. I just want some fried chicken, macaroni and cheese, and a waffle. Maybe some greens too. I keep hearing about this Roscoe's place, so I need to stack it up against Busy Bee's in Atlanta.

"Let's go!" I yell out the window while DeShawn is still talking to the driver. "I'm hungry!"

DeShawn climbs into the limo and slides over so that he's next to me. "You are sure impatient tonight, Sunday. You up here barking orders and stuff like you're a diva or something."

"I just have to get away from them, DeShawn! They are driving me bonkers, and I haven't had anything good to eat lately. Mystique has had me eating nasty little sour pieces of lettuce, and I need some soul food."

"My mother says you can fix the world's problems with good food."

I nod emphatically. "Your mother is right."

"What are you tripping on?" DeShawn asks.

"I don't know. Well, Sam got on my nerves tonight at the show. That 'she's my muse' crap was so played out, and not even fair. Now, to the world, he looks like the sweet and romantic boyfriend that I totally dissed. When I know the truth! He's the wretched and lying ex-boyfriend. He's the cheating and weed-smoking ex-boyfriend."

"And you show up on the red carpet with the dude from your video. Looks like you played him."

"Exactly. I so want to call up Jamie Foster Brown and do an interview with *Sister 2 Sister* magazine. She always has the real story."

"What would you say about your breakup? Would you put him out there like that? Would you give Jamie the whole scoop?"

"Good question. And I don't know the answer. It would depend on the day, I guess. Like right now, I would so put him on blast. But tomorrow, I might feel differently."

DeShawn nods his head thoughtfully. "So does he still have a chance? Like you're off him right now, but tomorrow you might feel differently?"

I feel DeShawn heading down a path where he's going to end up getting his feelings hurt.

"Man . . . I don't like being played. That won't change tomorrow, or the day after that."

"Okay, I hear you."

The limo driver pulls up in front of the restaurant and lets us out. I'd heard that if you came to this restaurant during their busy times that you have to stand in line. Luckily it's near midnight, so there's not much traffic.

DeShawn says to the limo driver, "Wait here. We should be about an hour."

"You want me to bring you some takeout?" I ask.

The limo driver smiles. "Yes, I would. The fried chicken breast, greens, macaroni and cheese, and candied yams."

"You about to eat all that this late at night?" I ask.

The limo driver nods. "I sure am!"

"That's what's up!" I give him a fist bump on the way into the restaurant.

After we've been seated and placed our orders, De-Shawn stares at me and chuckles.

"What is so funny?" I ask.

"You don't see how cool you are, Sunday. I don't know any other Grammy-award-winning R and B divas that would bring the limo driver dinner."

I laugh out loud. "You don't know any other Grammy-award-winning R and B divas at all!"

"Not true! I know Mystique, and she definitely wouldn't take the limo driver's order. She wouldn't care whether he ate or not."

I consider this and decide that I agree with DeShawn. Not only would Mystique not care about getting the driver food, but she'd want to know what nerve he had getting hungry on the job. She'd be mad if she heard his stomach growl. It would probably wreck her flow.

"Well, I guess that's just who I am. My mom says that everyone is important and that God is no respecter of persons. That's like her favorite scripture."

DeShawn says, "I agree with your mother."

"So what's your major, DeShawn? What are you going to do when we graduate from college?"

He shrugs. "I'm pursuing a dual major in political science and journalism. I'm thinking I can be one of those analysts on CNN."

"Wow. I had no idea."

"What, did you think I wanted to be an actor or something?"

I cover my mouth to stifle my laugh. "Yeah, I kinda did. I thought you were going to go from videos to movies and then make your home in Hollywood."

"You sound like you've got my career all planned out!"

"Okay, but I was totally and incredibly wrong. You want to be a news correspondent, not star in Tyler Perry movies!"

We burst into laughter that doesn't die easily. When one of us tries to stop, the other renews the flurry of giggles. We're still cracking up when our food finally arrives, but as soon as that crispy golden fried chicken and yummy thin and perfect waffle are in front of me, all laughter ceases.

"Are you going to eat all of that?" DeShawn asks.

I nod while trying to manage a huge mouthful of food. "I'm gonna dang sure try," I say after I swallow.

"That's just greedy."

"Have you tasted this? It'll give you a case of food lust that you wouldn't believe."

I grab DeShawn's fork and put a bit of waffle and chicken on it. Then I feed him the yummy morsel. He closes his eyes and moans.

"That was delicious," DeShawn says. "Do you want some of my macaroni and cheese? My greens are good too."

I don't wait for DeShawn to ask me again before digging into his plate and scooping up a forkful of food. It doesn't make any sense how delicious this is! I didn't expect it to come close to the Busy Bee Café, but they are certainly equals in my mind. Now I have East Coast and West Coast locations to indulge my greediness.

A pre-teenage girl has walked up to our table, and stands there with a notepad and pen in her hand. "Can I have your autograph?" she asks with a smile.

"She's eating," DeShawn says. "She'll do it before she leaves."

I narrow my eyes at DeShawn and take the girl's notepad. "Of course, I will give you an autograph. Did you watch the Grammys?"

The girl nods and grins. "I did! Congratulations on your award. You should've won the Best New Artist one too."

"Everybody keeps saying that! But I'm happy with the one I got. What's your name?"

"Aaliyah."

"Spelled like the singer?"

"Yes. She was my mom's favorite."

"My mom's too!"

I sign Aaliyah's notepad and then hand it back to her. "There you go."

"Thank you so much! Can I ask you a question?"

I nod. "Sure!"

"Who is this guy? Is he your bodyguard or something? Isn't Sam your boyfriend?"

DeShawn and I burst into laughter. "He is my bodyguard for the night, but mostly he's my friend," I say.

"Well, all of my friends love you and Sam! We watched the reality show where y'all fell in love. Will you tell him that Aaliyah from Los Angeles said hi?"

"I sure will. Thank you so much for your support."

"We love you, Sunday!" Aaliyah says, and all of her friends wave from their table.

"Love you more!"

Aaliyah walks or rather floats back across the room to her group of friends. DeShawn stares at me with a curious look on his face.

"What?" I ask.

"You didn't have to sign that right then. Next time you may not feel like it, and then people will say you don't appreciate your fans," DeShawn says.

"I do appreciate my fans, so that won't happen. If they want to line up around the block asking me to sign stuff, I'll do it. It's because of them that I'm a millionaire."

"Okay. Well, just make sure you don't have an off day. It'll be all over the blogs the very next day."

"I'm sick of worrying about the Internet bloggers."

"They are a blessing and a curse. They can help blow you up and destroy you at the same time. I guess that's why you need to go out with friends that sometimes double as bodyguards."

"Did that bother you?" I ask. "I didn't mean it in a bad way. You are watching out for me today."

"And I'd do it every day if you paid me. I'll be your bodyguard."

I scrunch my nose into a frown. "I don't think you're scary enough. Or big enough. I think I need a three-hundred-pound ex-NFL player or something."

DeShawn laughs. "I am not just a football jock. I'm a wrestler and I have black belts in jujitsu, kung fu, and karate. I can fight."

"Okay . . . you'll do for now. But just know that I'm looking to get a big dude on my squad. Some crazy guy tried to push up on me with his demo at the House of Blues in Atlanta. Sam saved me, but Sam is a one-punch kind of guy. If dude hadn't hit the floor, Sam might've been in trouble."

DeShawn lifts an eyebrow and juts his chin out defensively. "Sam still punching dudes over you?"

"Well, yeah. The guy was all on me, grabbing me and stuff. I'm glad he was there."

"I think he still wants to be with you, Sunday. I think he won't give up until he has you back."

I shake my head. "Nah, he knows that it's over. Anything else he feels is just leftover from when we were kicking it. There's no chance of us getting back together."

"That's what you say, but I don't think Sam agrees."

I shrug and take another bite of food before responding. "He doesn't have to agree in order for it to be true."

"I guess it doesn't matter what he thinks or believes, as long as he's not in my way when I make my move."

This makes me giggle. "Your move? Oh, boy! Will you do me a favor and warn me when this move is on the way?"

"I won't know ahead of time! But just know that when it comes it'll be perfect. It'll be the best move you ever had made on you."

Now my giggles change into snorts. DeShawn is hilarious! "You are the man, then! As a matter of fact, this move sounds dangerous. I hope I survive it."

"You got jokes, I see."

I try to make my face serious. I furrow my eyebrows and make my lips into a straight line. "I am being serious right now."

"Then why do you look like you're on the verge of cracking up?"

Since DeShawn easily sees through my façade, I just go ahead and laugh. "I'm sorry. I am feeling really silly tonight."

"Well, I like you silly, so it's all good."

He reaches across the table, covers my hand with his, and squeezes. My first instinct is to snatch my hand away, because it feels weird that he's not Sam. But the sincerity of his smile makes me change my mind.

I mean, even if I'm not ready for a new boyfriend, will it hurt anything to enjoy the attention of a really, really hot boy? No matter what your answer or any grown person's answer is, I'm gonna go with no—it won't hurt a dang thing.

13

———

I've got to finish this paper. I don't care what's going on with anyone, I've put this off long enough. I do not want to hear a lecture from my professor about priorities and about deciding what's important. I know what's important, but my first Grammy win was incredible!

Earbuds in. Laptop up. *A Mercy* here for reference. Pillows propped up on my bed. Today, I will complete this thing.

Why is Gia tapping me on my shoulder? Big, gigantic, internal sigh.

I snatch out the earbuds. "Yes? What?"

"Okay, don't get all fly with me, Grammy-award-winning Sunday Tolliver. I need to tell you something."

I roll my eyes. "How many Grammy references are you going to make?"

"I don't know. I guess I'll keep saying Grammy until I

am no longer irritated that you took DeShawn instead of me."

I chuckle. "Um . . . I needed someone who could wear a tuxedo."

"Whatever, Grammy winner."

"What did you want to tell me? I've got to finish this paper this week. Three days until it's due."

"How much have you written?"

"A paragraph."

"One paragraph on a five-page paper? That is so not a Grammy-worthy performance."

I kick my feet out in front of me and widen my eyes. "What do you want?"

Gia sighs and gets up from my bed. "Since the Grammy-award-winning Sunday Tolliver can't be bothered with her friends at the present, I guess I will go wandering around campus looking for someone to talk to."

My phone lights up with a text from Dreya. I'm outside your dorm. Let me in.

I give up! Will they leave me alone for just a few minutes? Just long enough for me to write my second paragraph on this essay?

I snatch out the earbuds once again and jump off the bed. I am to the door, just as the first knock lands.

"Who is that?" Gia asks.

"My cousin."

"Like don't we have security?"

"Somehow, she bypasses it every time," I say. "I think she's got a fan on the security crew."

I open the door, and Dreya is standing there with her hand on her hip. "What took you so long?"

I crack up laughing and step to the side so that she can walk in. "Why are you here, Dreya? I've seen more of you since you moved to New York City than when you lived here."

"Whatever. I'm here with Evan. He's got business. He's trying to sign one of Toni Braxton's sisters to a solo deal."

"Well, as you can see, I was studying, so make it snappy." I motion to the pile of papers and laptop on my bed.

Dreya crosses the room and plops down on the floor in front of my bed. "So, I overheard a conversation that I shouldn't have heard. Now, I don't know what to do."

"Was it Sam?" I ask.

Dreya frowns and shakes her head. "Okay, why would I be twisted over a conversation that lame had? No, it wasn't Sam. It was Evan and he was on a conference call with all of the heads at Epsilon Records."

"Ooh! What did you hear?" I ask. The homework can wait. Anything that went on in this conversation could provide useful information.

"Don't sound so excited. It's not good news. Epsilon Records is thinking of dropping me from my record deal."

"What? Why? You sold well with your debut, and now that you've dropped Truth and hooked up with Evan you're basically drama free."

Okay, that is a bit of a stretch. Dreya is never drama

free. She thrives on foolishness and creates it wherever she goes.

"I think Mystique is pulling the strings to get me dropped. She's mad about her hubby having a little child support check, and she thinks that I invited that chicken-head to her wedding reception. She's trying to destroy me."

"Mystique would never do that," Gia says.

Dreya slowly turns toward Gia with a stank look on her face. "Okay, who invited you to this conversation?"

"I don't need to be invited if it's taking place in my room."

"Get your girl," Dreya says. "She don't know me."

Gia says, "I can hear you! You can speak directly to me."

"Can you tell her she's not on my level, so I'll only speak to her through you?" Dreya says to me.

"Stop it, Dreya!" I say. "Gia, can Dreya and I please have a moment?"

"You're trying to kick me out of my own room, Sunday?"

Gia looks all kinds of angry. I definitely didn't mean to upset her, but I want to get Dreya out of here as soon as possible so I can finish my paper. Dreya's not leaving until she has her say about her Mystique conspiracy— and she's not having her say while she's arguing with Gia.

"I'm not trying to kick you out. I would never do that. I just want to hear Dreya out really quickly so *she* can be on her way and I can get back to my paper."

Gia shakes her head. "I'm gonna step out for a minute, and I'm doing it for you, Sunday. Not because your cousin came up in our room trying to regulate."

"Girl, bye. Ain't nobody heard that stupid speech but you."

Gia walks out of the room and slams the door behind her. Then she opens the door and slams it again.

For a long moment I don't say anything. I use the pause to choose my words carefully.

"Dreya. If Mystique is trying to get you dropped from your record deal, don't you think you somewhat deserve it for what you did to me?"

"Sunday, I was desperate. I didn't think they'd really drop you. I just wanted them to know how serious I was about my career. The stuff with Truth could've cost me everything."

"I hear what you're saying, but you'll understand if I don't want to get in this. It sounds like you need to go and make a truce with Mystique."

"Truce! Whatever. If I find out that heffa tried to get me dropped from the label, we are taking it to the mattresses. It's gonna be war."

I purse my lips together and shake my head. "It sounds like you already have your mind made up. So, I don't know how to help you."

"You can write me some banging songs, Sunday. I mean, every song has to be a number-one hit. We need to trash half the songs we've already done."

She says this like writing hit songs is the easiest thing ever. You can have all the right things—a great beat, perfect hook, and meaningful lyrics, and it still might not connect with people. And it has to connect in order to be a hit.

"Trash half the songs? Dreya, your record is set to drop in the summer. They're gonna want a listening party soon, and Epsilon will probably put out a single right after Bethany's record drops. We don't have time to trash half of those songs."

"So you want me to have a half-hot record."

"I want your record to be hot. I get paid if you sell a lot of records, even if you are shady as what. So, know that I'm going to give you the best that I got on this."

Dreya picks up a book from my bed, flips it over in her hands, and drops it on the bed. "How are you gonna give me the best? You're always rushing these days. Rushing to class, rushing to do some homework, rushing out on a date with your new boyfriend."

"I'm living my life. I'm doing what you do. I'm doing me."

"See, you don't even care if I get dropped from my record deal or not."

She's right. I don't care. I am a songwriter, so I can work with any hot artist Epsilon records signs. Even if it's Dreya's replacement.

But even if I don't care, my mom does. She'd want me to do this. She'd want me to help my raggedy cousin keep her record deal, because in her mind, that's what family would do. Luckily for Dreya, my mom means the world to me, and I don't want her to think she didn't raise me right.

"Look, Dreya, get Sam on the phone. Tell him to be here this weekend, starting on Friday. We lock ourselves in the studio until we have a hot record."

"And what about your homework?"

"I'll get it done. You just make sure Sam shows up, because that's the only way this is gonna happen in time."

"And who's gonna keep you two from killing each other?" Dreya asks.

"Hmmm . . . I think you better pray about that."

"Sunday, can I tell you something and you not get mad at me?"

See, I don't like when people ask me questions like this. The only reason why a person would preface a big reveal with a question like this is because it's going to make me mad.

"If it's going to make me mad, don't tell me. I've got work to do, and I don't feel like being all mad and twisted."

"Well, you shouldn't get mad, because it's not about you. It's something I'm thinking about doing, but I'm not sure about it."

I roll my eyes and lie down on the bed. "What is it, Dreya?"

"So, the other day I asked Evan if he was going to marry me."

My eyes widen. This should be good. "What did he say?"

"He didn't say anything. He just laughed."

I cover my mouth with my hand in shock. "What made you ask him that?"

"Well, I was out shopping with Evan's credit card, and of course, Evan had to call them and say that it was okay for me to buy whatever I wanted. And one of the heffas

that works there said that I was just like Julia Roberts in
Pretty Woman."

"Wow. Wasn't she a prostitute in that movie?"

"Exactly. And it really made me mad, so I said, 'I'm
not a trick, I'm Evan's woman. I live with him.' Then
both of the clerks in the store cracked up laughing like
they had some kind of private joke between them."

"Aw snap, I know you were embarrassed."

"I was, kind of, but then I asked them what they
thought was funny. And they said that every girl Evan
dated in the past five years said the same thing, but there
was always someone new. Then, one of the girls said, 'He
ain't the marrying kind, baby. Just get what you can and
keep it moving.' "

"And so that made you ask Evan if he was going to
marry you?"

"Yeah. I just wanted to see what he would say, and he
backed up what those cackling hens at the store said.
He's not thinking about marrying me. I'm just the flavor
of the month, or whatever."

"So now what?"

"I'm going to do what the ladies told me to do. They
said, get what I can and keep it moving."

"So, you're going to get him to buy you a lot of stuff?"

"Sunday, as smart as you are, you are really, really
dumb."

I kick Dreya in her big old butt with my foot. "Whatever. He's already launching your singing career; I mean
what more can you get from him?"

"I know a lot of stars that were hot for a minute, then

people stopped talking about them. Now they're doing reality shows still trying to get a check. I don't want that to be me."

"So, you don't want him to launch your singing career, and blow you up? I don't understand."

"I'm going to get Evan to give me a gift that keeps on giving."

I laugh out loud. "Okay, I must be dumb, because I have no idea what you are talking about."

"I'm gonna have Evan's baby, Sunday."

Oh my goodness. "Girl, stop! Stop it immediately. I'm calling Auntie Charlie right now, 'cause you done lost your mind. Don't you see what happened with Bethany?"

"Bethany is an idiot. She got pregnant by a high school senior. I'm not saying I agree with what she did, but I don't disagree either."

"Well, when do you plan on doing this?"

"My record is supposed to drop in May, and I really want that to happen. So, I guess after the record release."

"Good. Then I still have some time to talk you out of this foolishness."

Dreya shrugs. "It ain't foolish if it works. You got your millions, let me get mine."

Gia pops her head back into the room. "Um, are y'all gonna be done anytime soon? Because I've got to get dressed to go to the movies with my cousin."

"Yeah," Dreya says as she gets up from my bed. "Please, Sunday, don't say anything about this to anybody. I'm trusting you, so don't play me."

"I'm hoping that you change your mind, so I'm going to pretend you didn't say anything at all."

"Good, because I need you to come up with at least five new songs between now and the weekend. My bad, Gia. Thanks for letting me have my cousin to myself for a minute."

Gia nods. "Sure."

Dreya blows me an air kiss and leaves, and immediately Gia plops down on the floor in front of my bed.

"What was *that* about?"

"She's just living up to her name. Wants me to come up with a bunch of new songs for her record, like I'm some type of songwriting machine."

My phone buzzes. A text from Dreya. I just got you a present. You'll thank me later.

What is it? I text back, not sure if I want any of Dreya's surprises.

She replies, Just trust me, cuzzo. Xoxo

What does Dreya, the most suspicious person in the world, know about trust? Something tells me that I should do just the opposite of trusting Dreya. Something tells me I should be afraid.

14

Piper and I are standing in front of our dormitory mailboxes. She's looking for a check from her foster mom's church, and I wasn't expecting anything when I opened my box. Surprisingly, there is a big envelope, folded in half and shoved in my box. I take the envelope and flip it over in my hands. There's no return address in the upper corner, only my name and address in big block letters on the front, and a stamp that says PRIVATE.

"What's that?" Piper asks.

"I don't know. But I think I'm going to wait until I get back to my room to open it."

"Well, my check didn't come, so I'm ready to go back upstairs."

Piper's phone chimes and she giggles as she reads her text message.

"Are you going to share?"

She shakes her head as she types in a reply. "It's just

L.J. He's asking me what I'm doing . . . what I'm wearing. . . ."

"Ewwww!"

"Don't hate on me just because I have a boyfriend, Sunday. You could have one too if you stopped being so stubborn about DeShawn."

"I am not hating. I couldn't care less about you and your freaky guy."

"He's not freaky! He's just joking."

I poke my lips out in a "yeah right" gesture. "When are we gonna meet him anyway? We talked about doing a double date. When is that gonna happen?"

"I asked him about that, and he doesn't really have any homeboys that aren't with someone."

"All his homeboys are in relationships?"

Piper shrugs. "I guess."

"That's weird. Sounds like he just doesn't want to share you with anyone."

"Is that such a bad thing?"

"Not really, I guess."

As Piper and I walk to the stairs, we nearly collide with Meagan, who is walking and texting at the same time.

"Dang, Meagan," I say. "You should probably watch where you're going."

"I'm sorry. Linden was asking me what I'm wearing."

Piper giggles. "My boyfriend was just asking me the same exact thing."

"You both are dating freaks. Gross. Are your guys friends?"

Meagan shrugs. "I don't think so. He's never mentioned a James or L.J."

"And L.J. hasn't said anything about Linden. Is Linden a sophomore?"

"Yes, he is," Meagan says with a nod. "And he's about to pledge Chi Kappa Psi."

"James too! They've got to know one another," Piper says. "Maybe we should all get together, since I haven't really gotten to spend any time with you since we got back from winter break."

"Okay, let's do it. We should do brunch or something. See you later tonight? We can watch movies and girl talk."

"Really?" Piper asks. "You want to hang with me?"

"Of course! We're both dating Morehouse men, and it seems like we're going to be sorority sisters since you're determined to pledge Gamma Phi Gamma next year," Meagan says.

Meagan waves at us and bounces out of the dorm, and Piper's jaw drops in shock. "Can you believe that?"

I start up the two flights of stairs to our rooms. "Nope. But I guess having a boyfriend is a good thing for her, because she's totally a nicer person now that she's found her Morehouse man."

"Tell me about it. Maybe I can stop hanging in you and Gia's room now."

I give Piper a fake sad face. "We're going to be so sad about that."

"Whatever. I'm going to talk to my boyfriend. You can go do whatever it is that you do in that room, because it dang sure ain't homework."

I shake my head and roll my eyes at Piper as we part. I do, in fact, have homework to do. I have to put the final touches on my paper. I'm not in the mood to do it though. I've got music on the brain—song lyrics. But I try to push that out of my head, because if I don't get at least a B on this paper, I'm going to have a serious attitude.

I plop down on my bed with my mail, and start booting up my laptop. While the computer is going through its motions, I rip open the envelope. It's a stack of papers held together at the top with a paper clip. Initially, I think it's a contract, but it's not.

It's a paper on the themes of *A Mercy*. My homework assignment for composition class. There's a sticky note on the paper that says, *This one is on the house. If you like, contact me at paperwriter22@yahoo.com.*

I drop the papers like they're covered in poison. Is this Dreya's gift? I pick up the pages again and thumb through them. From what I can tell, it's well written. Heck, it's better than mine. Way better. This is an A paper in my hand.

If I didn't buy it, is it technically cheating if I turn it in?

Since I already know the answer to my internal question, I sit the paper down on the upper corner of my bed, in clear sight but out of immediate hand reach.

I send Dreya a text that says, Really, Dreya? Why would you buy me this?

A few moments later there is a response. Because I need u to stop playin and write my songs.

I toss the phone on the bed after reading Dreya's message. Then I pick up my notebook and write down the line that's been stuck on replay in my mind. *You never even knew me/You wanted me so bad/But what if I was the best thing/You never knew you had?/What if I left*

*you?/What if I said good-bye?/Would you keep it movin'
on?/Or would you be like/I loved her/Wish I had'a
treated her right.*

I feel a tiny smile on my face. This song isn't right for
Dreya. She'd never sing anything so sentimental. It's not
her style.

Deep down, I know where the lyrics are coming from.
My heart and mind kept trying to make sense of my
breakup with Sam, but it just doesn't make any sense,
and I can't make those remaining feelings go away.

I draw a few flowers in the corner of the page, and
then write another song snippet that I've been playing
with. *You can't compete/Hatin' on me/Keep askin' your-
self/How could it be/That I passed you up/Lookin' at
me/Givin' him somethin' he wants/Doin' all the things
you won't.*

Now this is a Dreya cut. I can imagine the track that
Sam might make for it. Staccato notes, with minimal
flourishes, hitting hard on the beat and looping over and
over again for effect. I don't have a doubt in my mind
that Dreya's going to like it.

After I get those two songs out of my mind for the moment, I feel like I can work on my paper a little. I scroll
through the pages and read what I've already written. I
type a few notes on the page that I think can help the
words flow better.

If only I was as good writing papers as I am at writing
songs.

I pick up the purchased paper again as Gia comes into
the room. I quickly shuffle the pages behind my back.

"What's up?" Gia asks. "You finish your stuff?"

"Uh, no . . . not yet."

"It's due day after tomorrow. Do you want me to look and see what you have so far? Maybe I can help."

I close my eyes and shake my head. I can't accept Gia's help or Dreya's. I pull the laptop onto my lap and snuggle into my big pillow.

"I'll be finished. I'm almost done."

"Okay, then, I'll be quiet if you want."

I nod and smile, then turn my attention to the computer.

A Mercy *is a piece of literature that studies motherhood. Can a woman be a mother without ever giving birth? In the world that Ms. Morrison has created, the physical process of pregnancy and childbirth don't always ensure that there is an eternal bond between mother and child. There are bonds that go dee . . .*

Suddenly, my computer screen goes blue and shuts down. "Crap! Crap! Crap!"

"What's wrong?" Gia asks.

"My computer just crashed."

"How much have you done today? Did you hit save?"

"I haven't even done that much today, so I'll just redo my edits. I'm glad I had saved it before."

I press the power button on my PC, and it does nothing. This is odd. I flip out the battery and put it back in, but the computer still doesn't boot up.

"Crap, crap, crap!"

"Still not working?" Gia asks. She gets up from her bed, plops down in front of mine, and takes the laptop from me. "Do you have a backup somewhere?"

"No. I didn't back it up. I meant to, but I never did. Do you think you can get it to work?"

Gia shakes her head. "It's not your battery. The power button in front shows that it's charged. It might be an operating system error, or some Trojan virus that deletes files from the hard drive."

"I don't know what that means! Tell me what that means!"

"It means that you're probably going to have to go back to your notes and piece together the sections."

"What notes? My notes are on the computer!"

"You don't have any notes in the margin of your book?"

"No!"

Gia slides down onto the floor in front of my bed. "Okay, I can help you put your paper back together. It's due on Thursday, so we've got two days to do this."

"Isn't there some computer geek that can rescue my computer from sudden death?"

Gia shrugs. "If there is, I don't know them."

"I have to turn in this paper, Gia! And I don't have time to start over from scratch. I've got a studio session tonight and one after class tomorrow."

"Can't you cancel one?"

I bite my lip and pull the pages from behind me. "I could . . . or I could just use this."

Gia frowns and snatches the pages from my hands. "Really, Sunday? You bought a paper? You're not a cheater. . . ."

"I didn't buy it. My cousin bought it for me."

"And *that* makes it okay? Didn't she miss out on graduating for cheating?"

"Wait, wait. I wasn't gonna turn the paper in as is. I was gonna rewrite it a little, switch some things around. . . ."

I don't even need Gia's judgmental frown to tell me that this is crazy talk. She's right. I am not a cheater, but I don't like failing either. I'm a winner.

Gia holds her hand out. "Give me that paper."

I hesitate for a moment, and clutch the paper a little tighter. "But . . ."

"But nothing. I'm gonna text Kevin and see if he has any computer geek friends. In the meantime, we're going to start reconstructing your paper. Together."

"I have to go to the studio."

She shakes her head firmly. "Not tonight. Call Big D and tell him you have an emergency."

"You're not the boss of me, Gia." I say this, but not with confidence. It feels like she is totally the boss of me right now.

Gia gently pries the paper from my hands. "I'm not the boss of you, but I'm your sister. What kind of sister would I be if I let you do this?"

I quickly swipe at my eyes to get rid of my tears. Gia is absolutely right to take this paper from me, and I would do the same thing for her.

"You think I don't know how you feel?" Gia asks. "I would be going crazy if I got two C papers in a row. But this can only get you in trouble."

"I know. I was only having a split second of crazy. I don't really want to cheat on this thing."

"Good!" Gia tears the purchased pages in a bunch of little pieces and lets them fall to the floor. "You're better than this. You are a Spelmanite, girl!"

"I am." I grab a notebook and pen from my bed and turn to a blank sheet.

I write a few words. *A Mercy is all about motherhood.*

Then, I let out a sigh. This is going to take all night. I send Big D a text. Tell Sam to get started without me. Sending a melody for him to work on.

I press the voice recorder on my phone and sing the little hook snippet that I wrote earlier for Dreya. This ought to hold them over for tonight, and I can have my paper done by tomorrow . . . if I stay up all night rewriting.

"That sounds hot," Gia says. "Is that what you were going to be working on tonight in the studio?"

"Yep. It's another song for Dreya's album."

Gia stands up and says, "If we're going to get this paper done, we need some power food. I'm gonna go and get your Starbucks, some chips, sandwiches, and Oreos. That ought to hold us."

"That sounds good. Especially the Oreos."

Gia smiles as she pulls on her shoes. "I know, right?"

As Gia grabs her purse and opens the door, I say, "Gia . . ."

"What's up? You want me to bring back something else?"

I shake my head. "No. I want to say thank you."

Her smile spreads even farther. "You're welcome, sister!"

15

I can barely keep my eyes open as Dreya belts out the hook that I sent to Sam last night. Gia and I didn't go to bed until five this morning. Gia even missed her morning class, but she said that it was okay; she'd borrow Piper's notes later.

At any rate, I've only had a few hours of sleep, but I still made it to my studio session. And why would Evan decide to pick this one time to show up? Every time I nod off he looks at me like I'm crazy.

"Looks like Sunday needs to lay off the frat parties, huh?" Evan says as I drift off once more.

"I did my part," I say as I wipe the drool from the corner of my mouth. "The song is written. The track is done. Dreya just has to sing it like she means it."

"I am singing it like I mean it."

Sam shakes his head. "No, you're not. This song is

perfect for you. You think the entire world is hating on you, so this is your anthem."

Dreya rolls her eyes. "Sometimes it feels like the entire world *is* hating on me."

"That! That's it," Big D says. "That attitude you just gave Sam. That's how you need to sing on this track. Take all that anger and get in the booth. We are about to do this right now."

Dreya gives Big D a little grin and then follows his instructions. I'm so glad she's in the booth. That's one song down, and four more to go.

"Where did this song come from?" Evan asks. "I don't think I've heard it before."

"You haven't," I reply. "I just wrote it yesterday. Dreya is not satisfied with her track listing."

"So we're spending more time and resources on a record that's already done?" Evan asks.

"I'm not charging her any extra for songs she doesn't use," I say. "She wants her album to go number one on the week it's released."

Evan shakes his head and sits down next to Big D. "I would love for her to have a number-one record, but Epsilon is pulling back the marketing dollars. She can have the best record in the country, but if no one knows about it, it won't go to number one."

"Why would they pull back dollars now on this project? Bethany is near platinum, and we've got a collaboration on here with Sunday and Bethany. This record is set to be a moneymaker."

"Y'all really don't know?" Evan asks. "Sunday, your girl Mystique is whispering in their ears over at Epsilon.

They desperately want to sign her to another contract after this next record, and she's playing hardball. She doesn't want them putting any money behind Dreya's project."

"She has that much power," Sam says. "I've seen everyone in a room scramble when she comes in, even Zac. They all want to give her exactly what she wants."

"Exactly," Evan says. "And she blames Dreya for that fiasco at her wedding. I wish I hadn't told Dreya about Zac's love child. I feel like it's my fault."

"You're the one who told her?" I ask. "Then it is your fault. And you need to fix it. How are you gonna make her record a number-one hit without any marketing money. You did it before Epsilon, now do it again."

The guys all look at me with strange expressions, like they don't understand why I'm so passionate about this. But they don't know Dreya's plans like I know them. If she only could have a number-one record, she might not try to saddle herself with Evan's love child. She wants so badly to have fame and fortune that she's in desperation mode. I don't want her there. I want her to enjoy this thing instead of stressing over it.

Evan rubs his goatee and nods slowly. "We could . . . leak some of her tracks. The ones we're not planning to use. They're really good, and it could get people wanting to hear more music from her."

"I don't like the idea of bootlegging my own music," Sam says. "There just seems like there's something not right about that."

I roll my eyes and laugh at Sam. He's got a sudden case of morality all of a sudden? Lying to his girlfriend and creeping in New York City didn't make it kick in, but up-loading a few throwaway tracks has him up in arms. He needs to miss the entire world with that foolishness.

"The songs belong to us, so it's not bootlegging," I say. "It's giving the fans a free gift. A gift that's gonna make them run out to buy Dreya's album on the day it's re-leased."

"And that's the gift that keeps on giving," Evan says. "Because when they buy, y'all get paid."

The gift that keeps on giving. That's what Dreya called the baby she plans to have with Evan. This plan has got to work! My mom would agree, although Aunt Charlie would probably want Dreya to have the baby.

"What y'all talking about out there?" Dreya asks through the microphone. "Y'all on my time, so it better be about me."

Evan smiles and presses the button to send his voice back to the booth. "We are talking about you. Your ears must be burning. We're talking about how to make you a star."

"I'm already a star. Let's do this."

Big D starts the track playing. Dreya closes her eyes and grabs the microphone like it's the last piece of chicken in the bucket and she hasn't eaten in days. This time, she sings the heck out of my song. She surprises me, really. I've never heard her sing this well.

Evan has a shocked, far-away expression on his face. That coupled with his wistful smile tells me that maybe he hasn't given up on Dreya, even if the heads of Epsilon Records have. This gives me a glimmer of hope that maybe my cousin can make her fortune on the mic and not by pushing a baby stroller.

After she's done singing, Sam gives Dreya a two-thumbs-up signal, and then speaks over the intercom. "That was hot, Drama. Come out here and listen to the playback. Rest your voice."

Dreya sashays out of the recording booth looking more than proud. She locks eyes with Evan and he reaches for her to pull her into his arms. He kisses her nose and then her mouth, and she beams. Is she in love with him?

"You *did* that," Evan says. "You sound like the queen of Reign Records up in this piece."

I clear my throat and poke my lips out. She ain't the queen at all.

Sam laughs. "You 'bout to start something up in here, Evan. Sunday looking real twisted right now."

"You're both queens," Evan says. "Bethany too. That's why we're Reign Records. We're taking over and running this industry. Every other label is gonna have to bow down."

"What about Mystique?" Dreya asks. "Is she gonna have to bow down too?"

"It's only a matter of time," Evan says. "If I don't do anything else in this industry, I'm gonna make sure that diva kisses your ring."

This causes Dreya to burst into a flurry of giggles. I don't join in on the laughter. I can't see myself at odds with my mentor, the one who gave me a career. This is not how I wanted this thing to turn out. Why can't we all be queens? Why does anyone have to bow down?

Sam walks over to the keyboard bench where I'm sitting, and he crowds my space by plopping down next to me. My first thought is that I should jump up and run to the other side of the room, but he smells so good. I know he's purposely wearing my favorite cologne, just to mess with me. I notice he's got a new tattoo on his neck. A tiny treble clef.

"You got a new tat," I say. "Please don't tell me you're gonna be one of those dudes covered in ink."

He stares at me with an intense gaze. No smile anywhere to be found. It makes me uncomfortable, and my heart races a little.

"Nah," he finally replies. "I won't get covered with ink, but I do have one I think you'll like."

He rolls up his shirt sleeve and shows me the writing on his (bulging) bicep. It says, in tiny script, *Muse*.

Muse? I am his muse . . . so he says. So is that supposed to be for me? I swallow even though my mouth is bone dry. I will not let him get to me.

"When did you get that?" I ask.

"The week before the Grammys."

I don't comment on what I know it means. "Yep. You're already starting down that road. Next thing you'll have one of those Mike Tyson tats on your face."

"It would be an improvement," Dreya says. She high-fives me as we burst into laughter.

Big D says, "That was a straight-up hater move."

"I got my cousin's back," Dreya says. "Speaking of which, how did you like my present?"

"Um . . . thanks but no thanks. I don't need that."

"Don't need what?" Evan asks.

"Nothing. It's between us," Dreya says. "We're cousins. We're allowed to have secrets. Isn't that right, Sunday?"

Dreya winks at me to let me know that she's talking about *all* of our secrets, including her ridiculous baby-making plan. Guess I haven't convinced her yet that she doesn't need to do this.

I respond to Dreya's wink with a gigantic sigh and (my mom would be happy to hear this) a tiny, silent prayer.

16

_____

"Coffee. Just a cup of coffee." I close the IHOP menu and hand it to the waiter. After I got back in from the studio last night, Gia was up and ready to work on my paper with me. We worked all night long!

Gia, who is sitting across the table from me, frowns. "Is that all you're going to have for breakfast?"

"I'm too tired to eat," I moan. "I just want to turn in this paper and go to bed for twenty-four hours. For real."

"Why don't you do just that? After class you should just get some rest. Turn off your phone and go to sleep. Not for twenty-four hours though."

Piper walks into the restaurant and slides into the booth next to Gia. "Did y'all order yet?"

Gia nods. "We just did. I got the strawberry crepes, but Sunday only got coffee."

"Ewwww. You need a coffee detox. As soon as you finish Dreya's album, I think you should go on a raw diet with me."

"Raw diet?" I ask.

"Yep. All of the foods will be in their natural state. We can do some juicing and soak oats in water for breakfast. We'll have raw granola and fruit for snacks."

This sounds nasty. "No thank you, Piper. I know you mean well, but I am so not interested in doing that."

"Suit yourself. When you start getting wrinkles and laugh lines you'll wish you'd listened to me."

I laugh out loud. "Gia, will you tell this girl something? Black don't crack."

"That is true, Piper. Black women age well. We don't start getting laugh lines and stuff until we're in our forties."

Piper laughs and shakes her head. "Really? Well, enjoy your disgusting coffee then."

"It's delicious. It's black gold," I say.

But Piper isn't looking at me anymore. She's staring at the door of the restaurant with her mouth hanging open. I turn around in my seat to see where she's looking, and I see Meagan walk in the door with another girl and two guys.

"Oh, look," Gia says. "Meagan is here. Wave her over so we can finally meet her boyfriend!"

"I-I . . ." Piper can't seem to open her mouth, so Gia waves her arms in the air.

"Meagan!" Gia yells. "Over here!"

Meagan smiles and waves. Then she grabs one of the

guys' hand and walks over to the table. I guess that this is Linden, and he is fine! But, wait. Why is he looking at Piper like he's just seen a ghost?

"Hey, you guys!" Meagan says. "So finally, I guess I'll let you all meet my boyfriend, Linden. So . . . girls this is Linden, and Linden this is Gia, Piper, and Sunday, who I'm sure you already know from television."

"When you introduced yourself to me," Piper says, "you told me your name was James. And that everyone calls you L.J."

"James is my middle name. And my friends back home call me L.J."

Meagan has a confused look on her face. "L.J.? Your *boyfriend* L.J.?"

"Yes. It looks like we're sharing a Morehouse man."

"Linden!" Meagan cries. "What is she talking about?"

"Meagan, babe, I can explain. I met both of you around the same time. I didn't know that she was your friend, and of course we weren't exclusive at first."

Meagan snatches her hand away from Linden. "W-when did you find out?"

"Just last week. I've been trying to break it off with her ever since we decided to be exclusive."

Piper cocks her head to one side angrily, and whips out her cell phone. "Is this how you break up with someone? You send them a text that says, 'What are you wearing beautiful? Can't wait to see you.' That doesn't sound like breaking up to me. Does it sound like breaking up to you, Gia?"

Gia's eyes widen. I don't think she wants to get in this conversation, because she doesn't say anything.

"What you think, Sunday? Huh? Does that sound like breaking it off?"

I touch Piper's hand. "Piper, don't. Let's talk this out later, not here in public."

"But he's right here, Sunday. We're all together. He won't let this happen again." Piper has black eyeliner-tinted tears streaming down her face and the hand that I'm holding is shaking.

"So, you've been seeing her this whole time?" Meagan asks. I find it strange that she won't speak at all to Piper. She won't even look at her.

"Not really. I've been out with her a couple of times. Once I found out you were roommates, I wanted to let her down easy. I didn't want to come between the two of you."

"Well, you were doing the right thing," Meagan says. "Because now, I can't see myself being her roommate anymore. It'll be strange with me dating someone she obviously likes."

"You're going to keep dating him?" Piper asks. "How could you?"

Meagan says, "We just got serious, Piper. I don't expect a guy to be exclusive until we're exclusive. And I'm not mad at you. You didn't know. But it won't really be fair to you for us to be roommates anymore. I'll talk to our resident advisor."

Piper jumps up from the table and gets right in Meagan's face. "You would choose a guy over me. That is so like you."

"Well, we really just met this year. It's not like we go way back or anything like that. We hardly know one another."

Linden or James, or whatever the heck his name is, puts his hand around Meagan's waist and pulls her close. She tosses her straight hair over her shoulder and lets him kiss her bare neck.

"I'm so sorry you had to find out like this," Linden says. "Sorry, Piper. I didn't mean to hurt you."

Piper storms out of the restaurant, leaving the rest of us with the uncomfortable situation.

"That was crazy," Meagan says echoing my thoughts. "Come on, Linden. I'm starved, and we've left our other friends waiting."

I watch in shock as Linden and Meagan walk away . . . hand in hand.

"What just happened?" Gia asks me.

"I have no idea. I was just about to ask you that."

Gia looks behind her at Meagan laughing and joking with the Gamma Phi Gamma crew. "So, she's okay with this?"

"She's probably just keeping her cool," I say. "I'm sure she just wants to confront him in private."

But then, Meagan shoots that theory totally out of the water by throwing her arms around Linden's neck and kissing him sweetly on the cheek.

"Yep. She's confronting him all right," Gia says.

"We should go after Piper and make sure she's all right." I stand up from the table and don't wait for Gia to answer. It's not even necessary, because I already know she's going to follow.

On our way out of the restaurant, Meagan calls to us. "I'll drop by your room later, okay?"

"I think we'll already have company, Meagan," I say. "Maybe you should keep hanging with your future sorors."

"We're hoping that you too will consider Gamma Phi Gamma," Peony, head of the Gamma clique says.

"I hadn't really considered it. Don't know if I'm the sorority type."

Peony lets out a shrill giggle. "Every girl is the sorority type. They either get chosen or they don't."

My only response to this is a half-smile. Gia says nothing at all either, and we leave IHOP together.

"You still thinking about pledging Gamma Phi Gamma?" I ask Gia as we get into the car.

"Nope. I think we should start our own sorority."

"What would we call it?"

"Beta Kappa Fly!"

"That's what's up!" I say with a laugh. "Let's go find our other soror before she gets another tattoo, or busts some windows out of somebody's car."

Gia and I burst into laughter, trying to laugh really hard about something that's not funny at all. I haven't forgotten how my girls sat up all night long with me when I had a broken heart over Sam. Now it's time for me to repay the favor.

17

We find Piper sitting on the floor outside our room. Her knees are pulled up to her chest and she's hugging them tightly. I don't see tears in her eyes, but her face is red with anger.

"Piper, you okay?" Gia asks.

She shakes her head. "No. I am not okay."

Gia and I sit down on either side of Piper. Gia puts her arm around Piper's shoulders and I take her hand in mine.

"I'm madder at Meagan than him. You expect boys to be play games, but not your sister."

"Was she really your sister though?" Gia asks. "It seems like you two never really hit it off that well."

"We were getting closer, though. At least I thought that we were." Now the tears come from Piper. "We were swapping boyfriend stories every night."

"Dang, that's messed up y'all were talking about the same dude," I say. "Like it wasn't sounding familiar at all?"

Piper nodded. "Some things *did* sound similar, like how we used to always get back-to-back text messages. But I knew that my boyfriend's name wasn't Linden."

Gia stretches her legs out in front of her and says, "I know he said that he didn't know y'all were roommates, but why would he give y'all different names? It just seems strange."

"I think he was just being a player type," Piper says. "I can't imagine someone being that mean on purpose."

I don't have anything positive to say on that subject, so I keep my comments to myself. I do, indeed, think that boys can be that mean on purpose. Sometimes they feel bad afterward, but they definitely are some of the most selfish beings on the planet.

"So what are you gonna do, I mean about the room-mate situation?" I ask, changing the subject from Linden James's chicanery.

Piper sighs. "I guess I'm going to get a new roommate, but I don't want that! What if the new person is messy?"

"What if she smells bad?" Gia asks.

"What if she snores and farts in her sleep?" I can barely get my question out without giggling.

Piper pinches both of us. "You two are not kind. If I get a roommate like that I'm going to move in with y'all."

"It's like you already live with us anyway," I say. "You're at our dorm every day and you eat all of the food in my mini-refrigerator. Speaking of which, did you eat my macaroni and cheese? I was looking forward to smashing that."

"Um, no! I don't like your noodles and lard. I would never eat that," Piper says.

Gia raises one finger in the air. "I'm sorry. That was me. I was hungry, and my pizza was nasty."

"Greedy is your middle name. Gia Greedy Stokes. That's your name," I say.

"Hold up, hold up, hold up," Piper says. "I remember Sunday said she was moving us into an apartment next year. Do we have to wait? Can't we move off campus now?"

I shrug. "I guess so. I haven't been condo shopping, though. I've been putting it off."

"We need somewhere with a pool," Gia says. "And a game room. And an office."

"All that?" I ask.

"And a Jacuzzi?" Piper asks.

"You two are out of control, but it might be fun to go house shopping. I've hardly spent any of my money."

"Are you serious?" Gia asks. "Well, why don't we go to the mall?"

"I'm broke, so shopping won't be much fun for me," Piper says.

"Well, I'm between blessings myself, but we gotta do something other than sit around here," Gia says.

"Between blessings?" Piper asks. "That's church speak for . . . ?"

"Broke. It is church speak for broke," I say with a laugh. "Let's go. I'll buy y'all an outfit."

Just as we start down the stairs, DeShawn and Kevin are coming up.

"Sunday! You haven't been checking your texts," Kevin says in an irritated tone.

Okay, he is definitely on one hundred right now, and I need him to bring it on down to at least two.

"Kevin, what are you tripping on?" I ask.

"Did you forget that you have a photo shoot for *Vibe* magazine with the entire Reign Records crew? It starts in two hours, but you have to get down to the aquarium for hair and makeup."

"The aquarium? Is the entire Reign Records crew gonna be there or just the artists?"

Kevin scrolls through his messages. "Um . . . Evan, Big D, and Sam are going to be there too."

Shoot, shoot, shoot. I do not want to go anywhere near the aquarium with Sam. That is the place where we had our first date, and our first kiss. That will bring up too many hurtful memories.

"I guess we're going to have to postpone our shopping trip, y'all. I've got to go to work."

"Are you ready to go?" DeShawn asks.

"Yes, but why are you going? Kevin is my assistant."

DeShawn gives me an annoyed pout. "I'm your body-guard, or did you forget about the guy that tried to take you out at House of Blues?"

"I didn't forget about him. Come on then."

My decision to let DeShawn come with me to the photo shoot has more to do with me being uncomfort-able around Sam at the aquarium than the fear of any overzealous aspiring artists. I hope that if Sam sees me come in with DeShawn then maybe he'll assume we're together and not try to push up on me.

When I walk into the aquarium with my "entourage" everyone else is already here.

Dilly runs up to me and gives me a bear hug. "What's going on, stranger? You haven't called a brotha or nothing!"

"I've been super busy, Dilly-Dill."

"I know, but I still miss you."

Bethany waves at me, but it doesn't look enthusiastic or friendly. In fact, her facial expression is totally blank even though there's a small smile on her lips. She looks like she's in a trance.

"She just took a Xanax," Dilly says. "She said photo shoots stress her out."

"A Xanax? Who gave it to her?" I don't know why I think Evan is her drug supplier, but I do.

"She pulled it out of her purse. It was in a prescription bottle."

"Hmmm . . . not good."

Dilly shrugs. "Maybe she really is stressed out."

"Yeah, the music industry is kind of harsh," Kevin says.

I wouldn't say that the industry is being very harsh to Bethany. Her record debuted at number one, and her video of the single she did with Dilly is in heavy rotation on MTV and BET. Her next single is the collaboration I wrote for me, Bethany, and Dreya. Evan thinks it'll be a number-one hit. She should be feeling really good right now.

"Come on," Kevin says. "You need to go to hair and makeup."

"I'm so mad that he is such a good assistant," De-Shawn says. "How do you know she needs to go to hair and makeup, fool?"

Kevin laughs. "She's here for a photo shoot. Duh!"

I scan the room and take in what everyone else is wearing. The theme, I'm guessing, is royalty. Everyone has on something red, purple, or white. I don't see Sam, so he must not be here yet. Anjelica, Evan's stylist from New York, is running back and forth with fabric swatches and shoes in her hands.

Anjelica runs up to me and says, "I have the perfect dress for you, sweetie! Tell the hairstylist that I said to give you a curly updo!"

I don't even have time to nod my response, before Kevin is ushering me over to the stylist's chair. This time the hairstylist is a guy. He's a total hottie with his baggy pants, fitted sweater, and Timberland boots. He's got incredible swag.

He motions toward the chair. "Sunday, I'm Ron, and I'm pleased to be doing your hair for this photo shoot. Do you know what you're wearing?"

"Not exactly, but Anjelica said that my hair should be in a curly updo."

Ron nods. "Gotcha. You are gonna be sexy as what when I'm done. But let's get this gel catastrophe washed out of your head."

As Ron leads me away, Kevin says, "Do you need me to do anything else?"

"No. Thanks, Kev. You're awesome."

I follow Ron to the sink in the back of our staging area. Then, I see him. Sam is in the back of the ballroom with his arm around a girl who looks like the ultimate groupie. Her tube dress barely covers her massive breasts and thick legs. When she sees me, she smiles and turns to give me a view of her backside—also ridiculously disproportioned to her tiny waist. Sam gazes over at me and gives me a head nod.

I swallow hard to keep myself from vomiting all over the place. I thought I could handle seeing Sam with someone else, but my stomach is turning cartwheels.

"I'm sorry that this isn't exactly five star, Sunday," Ron says. "But this is the best I could do."

I take a seat in the tiny chair in front of the sink and reply, "Most of the time, I wash my hair in the shower, so this is okay with me."

As I lean back in the chair and allow Ron to scrub all of the gel and dirt from my hair, I squeeze my eyes shut—not to keep out the shampoo, but to hold in the tears. I don't want anyone to see them, especially Sam and his Jessica Rabbit doll.

I knew that Sam would move on. He's a guy, and guys do that. They don't stay sad about a girl for long before moving on to the next one. But how could he say that I am his muse, and then show up here with another girl? I don't think he meant that at all. Those were only words, because he wanted to get back together with me.

Ron makes quick work of my product-filled hair and wraps it with a warm towel. "That feels good," I say.

"I microwave them. Makes it seem a little classier for you rich folk."

"I'm not rich. Not yet."

Ron bites his bottom lip and looks me up and down. "Really? You sold a bunch of records. If you ever need a hairstylist to go on the road with you, let me know. I'm available."

Somehow I don't think his "I'm available" has anything to do with styling my hair. He's looking at me like how the wolf licked his chops at Little Red Riding Hood.

"I'm not planning any tours right now, but give me your card, and I'll make sure to call you if I do."

"That's what's up. Come on, and let me finish making you beautiful."

"Sunday!" Sam calls from across the room. "I've got someone I want you to meet."

I act as if I don't hear Sam and speed up my steps toward Ron's styling chair. I think Ron can tell what I'm doing, because he starts laughing.

"We don't have to hurry, Sunday. We've got another hour before we start shooting," Ron says.

Sam catches up to us as I plop down into the chair and throw the cape over my body.

"Oh, hey, Sam," I say nonchalantly as if I'm just now noticing him.

Sam says, "Sunday, this is my new friend Phoebe. Phoebe, this is Sunday Tolliver."

Phoebe gives me a huge smile. "Sunday, I'm such a huge fan of yours. I would love to make you a piece of jewelry. Can I?"

"Jewelry?" I ask.

Sam says, "Pheobe makes custom jewelry out of crystals, diamonds, platinum, and gold. Look at this ring she made me."

Sam holds out his hand to show me the diamond encrusted S on his right hand. It's big and gaudy—totally different from the style Sam *used* to have. He's gone to New York and let Zac and Evan turn him into a true hip-hop baller.

"Uh . . . this isn't really my style," I say.

Phoebe giggles. "I wouldn't make you something like this, silly! I'd make you something tiny and feminine. How about I make you a prototype with cubic zirconium and silver? If you like it then I can do the real thing."

"Uh, I guess that would be okay."

"Great! I'm going to go out to the car and get my portfolio. Maybe you'll see something in there that you want."

Phoebe runs, or jiggles out of the ballroom, capturing the attention of Ron and Sam. Ron even drops the comb on the floor. Guys are disgusting.

"Is she your new girlfriend?" I ask Sam.

He nods. "Yeah. She's really nice."

I don't know if I expected him to lie or make up some excuse, but I did not think he'd say she was his girlfriend.

"Good for you."

Sam lifts an eyebrow and gives me a strange look. I would add something else, but Ron is pulling a hot blow dryer through my thick hair. I can just feel my hair strands being damaged. I'm gonna start rocking wigs at these things.

"You're cool with it?" Sam asks. "I thought you'd be mad."

Ron turns off the blow dryer and I clear my throat. "No. I was mad when you lied to me about Rielle. I was mad about you making out with a random chick at the club. You're not my man anymore, so why should I be angry about you dating someone?"

Sam places a finger on my chin and tips my face up. "Nah, not angry, but sad maybe."

"Boy, please, you need to stop feeling yourself. Can't you see that I brought DeShawn with me? We both brought our new boos."

"So you *are* dating DeShawn. I wondered when you were going to come clean about that."

"I don't answer to you, so it's whatever." It's hard to keep a straight face because Ron is furiously sticking pins into my hair to pin it up.

"Hey, Sam, you're already dressed for the shoot," Ron says. "Can you please have this conversation with Sunday after I get her all glammed up?"

Sam nods and saunters off toward Big D, Evan, and the rest of the crew.

"You are not believable at all, Sunday," Ron says. "But, I don't think Sam is being real either. I don't think he's with Phoebe."

"Really? Why do you say that?"

Ewww. Did I really just sound all eager and pressed like that?

"Well, I happen to know Phoebe from around the way, and Sam isn't really her type. He's not rich enough."

"Well, Sam isn't poor."

"The last man Phoebe dated was a Persian sheik."

"A for-real sheik?"

"Yep. He's the one who launched her jewelry company. She's still dealing with him sometimes, but he's married, so it's on the low-low."

I roll my eyes and poke out my lips. "If it's so on the low how do you know about it?"

"Hairstylists get all the gossip. It's like people sit in my chair and all of a sudden get diarrhea of the mouth."

"Well, then I have nothing else to say."

Ron laughs out loud. "Don't tell me anything else then, even though I helped you out. You still digging Sam, and I just let you know the door is still open."

"Now, that's where you're wrong. I don't want to get back with him, but I was feeling some kind of way about him having a new girlfriend."

"What's wrong with your cousin?" Ron pulls my head up and points over at Dreya, who runs to a garbage can in the corner and falls to her knees.

"Is she throwing up?"

I jump out of the chair with my hair half finished and run over to Dreya.

Anjelica yells at me. "Sunday! Let me tend to her. You need to get your hair finished, so we can start."

"Yeah," Evan says. "She'll be okay. She just partied a little too hard last night."

I cut my eyes at him as I help Dreya to her feet. I motion across the room to Kevin and he rushes over.

"What do you need?" Kevin asks.

"Can you get her some water? She's not feeling well."

Dreya wipes her mouth with a napkin and whispers, "I don't have a hangover."

"Then what's wrong with you?"

She mouths the words, *You know.*

Oh my goodness. She just told me about this whole getting pregnant thing last week. Had she already done it?

"I'm okay, y'all. Sunday, I'm gonna rinse my mouth out while you get your hair done."

Big D has a concerned look on his face, and then he frowns in Evan's direction. Big D was never for Dreya going to live with Evan in New York City. And it didn't even make sense anyway, because they are back in Atlanta every other week. I wonder if Evan is charging all these plane tickets against Dreya's royalties.

I trudge back over to the chair to finish getting glamorfied. After Ron finishes my hair (which has enough bobby pins to set off a metal detector), the makeup artist, a girl named KiKi, sprays foundation and bronzer on my face.

"Let that dry for a few minutes," KiKi says.

Anjelica brings me a white tube dress and red heels. The dress is over-the-top sexy, and not my style, but for some reason I feel like looking hot.

When I squeeze myself into the tube dress, I realize how little it actually is. It makes me look like I have long legs and I kind of wish I had a robe or long coat. From the way Sam and DeShawn's eyes bulge out, I'm guessing the desired effect was achieved.

DeShawn whistles. "You look smokin' hot, Sunday!"

The photographer, a guy named Jacinto, starts moving people around in poses as I run over to the randomly placed furniture. The first pose has Big D in a big purple armchair with a crown and a cane looking like Notorious B.I.G.'s twin.

"Girls, surround Big D. Make it seem like you want to call him big daddy," Jacinto says.

Dreya scrunches her nose. "Um, but we don't want to call him that, so I'm sure I'm gonna look really fake on this picture."

This makes me burst into laughter, and Bethany crack a half-smile. Her former self would've been laughing too, but this overly medicated person obviously doesn't have too many emotional outbursts.

Jacinto takes a few shots while we're getting ready, and then a few once we're posed. Then, all of the guys pose together. Sam and Dilly stand back to back, and Evan and Big D sit in side by side thrones.

"Try not to look like y'all are in prison," Jacinto says. "Can I have some softer facial expressions? I know y'all are hip hop and everything, but just don't give me criminal."

Jacinto's commentary is hilarious, and so on point, because I was totally thinking that they looked like one of those photos people take with their family members in prison. Especially Dilly and Sam with that back-to-back thing.

"Now, I want Sunday and Drama together. I want Sunday to wear a crown and give me all that bubbly happiness she always brings, and Drama, you give her the side-eye whatever kind of look."

Dreya frowns. "Everyone always wants me to play the hater role. I don't hate on Sunday."

Jacinto pauses and taps the side of his camera. "Just this once, I will accept feedback. Switch. Sunday, you play the hater in this one."

I smile, and hand Dreya the crown. I give so much attitude in my poses that Jacinto actually squeals. He's loving it.

"See, I told y'all Sunday was just a big ol' hater!" Dreya says. "Look how well she does this."

"It's called acting," Big D says, "and Sunday is good at it. I think I'm going to have you audition for a few roles."

"I want to get the Reign Records Romances," Jacinto says. "So, I'm going to pair Sam and Sunday, Evan and Drama and Bethany and Dilly."

"But Bethany and I aren't together at all," Dilly protests.

"Sam and I are broken up," I say, "so I don't think that counts as a romance either."

Jacinto taps his camera again. "Bethany and Dilly will stand in a 'baby, baby, please' type of pose."

"What?" Dilly asks.

"Get down on one knee and gaze up at her like you're begging. Bethany, I want you to look indifferent. You don't care about what he's saying."

Well, that's going to be easy for Bethany. She looks like she doesn't care about anything at all right now. Dilly is fuming, but he plays along anyway.

"Now, Dreya, I want you to sit in Evan's lap, looking toward the ceiling with your back arched and one leg kicked up. Evan, you stare at her with longing in your eyes."

Evan laughs out loud. "She should be staring at my pocket with longing in her eyes."

"Are you saying I'm with you for your money?" Dreya asks.

"Maybe not *just* for the money, but yeah. If I was a regular dude you wouldn't have given me any play."

Dreya laughs. "You're right. But I don't date regular dudes—only bosses."

Jacinto snaps photos through their entire conversation. I want a photo album of his candid shots!

"Right before the group photo, I want Sam and Sunday together. It should be a profile shot, and I want Sam standing with his hands in his pockets looking down at Sunday. Sunday, kick off your high heels, place both hands on Sam's chest, and stand on your tiptoes. Part your mouth, like you're in awe of him."

I clear my throat and look at the sky for a second. Then, I give myself a pep talk. I'm a professional, I can do this. It's just Sam. I really liked him once, so I should be able to do this.

I glance over at DeShawn to see if he even cares, but he's chatting it up with Kevin and playing with his cell phone. He's in the business, so he knows that a photo shoot is just that—a photo shoot. It's not real.

So, I shake off my issues, and kick off my shoes. "Come on, Sam," I say. "Let's give them some Reign Records romance."

Is that a glimmer of hope I see on Sam's face? I'm not sure, because as quickly as it came it disappeared.

I play up my part and lift an eyebrow as I gaze at Sam with parted lips. Sam's expression is nothing but melancholy and sadness. It is the opposite of romantic. But I guess it works because Jacinto is squealing again about how hot these poses are.

Sam jumps when I place my hand on his chest. My touch seems to make him nervous.

"Hold that!" Jacinto yells.

And Jacinto snaps away, capturing this awkward moment between me and Sam. While everyone else cheers about what great models we are, I know that neither one of us is acting. Sam is tripping so much on us not being together that he pretended to have a girlfriend.

And I pretended not to care.

18

It's early in the morning when I get the call to go to the dean's office. I can't think of a reason why Dr. Whitacre would want to see me, other than me paying Piper's tuition bill. That was supposed to be a secret, though, so that's probably not it.

I quickly get dressed in a knee-length skirt, cardigan, thick tights, and boots. It's nearing the end of winter, but this morning there's a chill in our room letting me know that it's even colder outside.

Ten minutes later, after a brisk walk across campus, I'm in Dr. Whitacre's waiting area trying to warm my nose and hands.

I notice that there are three other girls here, dressed in similar outfits and looking as confused as I am. The one sitting next to me is shaking and has tears rolling down her cheeks.

The crying girl asks me, "Did you get a phone call this morning to come here?"

"Yes, did you?"

"I did. My mother's going to kill me if I lose my scholarship."

Both my eyebrows rise in surprise. "Wait a minute. You know what this is about?"

"You don't? This girl on campus got busted for selling papers. Dean Whitacre is calling in anyone who's associated with it."

"But I didn't buy any . . ." Of course. The *gift* that Dreya gave me has come back to haunt me. Dang, dang, dang!

The crying girl bursts into tears again. "There's just so much pressure, you know! I have to get good grades or I lose my scholarship."

I try to shush her. With a thing like cheating, admitting that you succumbed to the pressure of college life isn't really a good argument. She needs to come up with a better story than that.

"They don't have any proof, do they?" I ask.

Crying girl shakes her head. "Only Natalie's word on who she sold the papers to."

When the door to Dr. Whitacre's office opens, a girl walks out looking completely devastated. There are tears rolling down her face, and she can't stop sobbing.

"But I want to be a Spelmanite!" crying girl number two wails. "I can't go to community college!"

The first crying girl jumps up from by my side and runs out the office like she's being chased by brain-eating zombies. Leaving me as the next person to enter Dr. Whitacre's office.

I take timid steps into Dr. Whitacre's office and stand in the doorway, trying to gauge her mood. She looks furious, like her head is going to spin right around on her neck. Her glasses are perched right on the tip of her nose, and her bun has so many stray hairs hanging loose, that she looks like she got up and kicked the last girl's behind.

"Close the door behind you and come sit down," Dr. Whitacre says.

I do what she says, and slowly take a seat in the hard wooden chair in front of her desk.

"Do you know why you're here, Ms. Tolliver?" Dr. Whitacre asks.

I shake my head, although now I have an idea. "I don't think so."

"Last week, there was a report about a young woman on campus who was selling papers to her sister Spelmanites. When I brought her in for questioning, she admitted her wrongdoing and named you as one of the recipients of the purchased compositions. What do you have to say about this?"

First of all, can I just say that I understand now the whole purpose of the interrogation room on *Law & Order* and every other cop show my mother loves to watch on TV? I feel as if Dr. Whitacre already knows all of the answers and that her only job is to try to catch me in a lie.

"I did receive one of the papers, however, I did not purchase it, nor did I turn it in. I am not a cheater."

Dr. Whitacre narrows her eyes at me as if she's trying

to see right through me. I can tell that this is not the answer she expected.

"Really? Then how do you explain this?" Dr. Whitacre slams my most recent assignment from Mrs. Due's class on the desk in front of me. "Your professor says that this is the first paper you've submitted that wasn't mediocre."

"That is true. This is the first paper in her class that I spent time and effort on. I even had to rewrite it from memory two days before it was due because my computer crashed."

"Even if this is your work, there's still the matter of you purchasing one of the papers."

I clear my throat and exhale calmly. "I did not purchase the paper. My cousin, who doesn't even attend Spelman or any other institution of higher learning, bought the paper and sent it to me as a gift."

"That is a very convenient story, Ms. Tolliver."

"Convenient and true."

"You're dismissed, Ms. Tolliver. Send in the next girl."

"That's all?"

She nods. "Yes. I don't have proof that you purchased this paper. All of the other girls have admitted to their cheating."

I stand from my seat. "I'm sorry to even be associated with this, and I told my cousin that I did not appreciate her purchasing a paper for me."

"You should also know that I not only take cheating very seriously, but lying as well. If you are not telling the truth, it would only help you to come clean right now. If I find out that you're lying, you will surely be expelled."

In this moment, I understand suspects who lie and say

that they committed a crime. I almost feel compelled to make up a story so that Dr. Whitacre can be right.

Instead, I say, "I understand."

A chill runs down my spine as I walk out of Dr. Whitacre's office. I can't believe how close I came to using that paper. If it hadn't been for Gia talking some sense into me, I might be getting kicked out of school right now. Talk about something not being a good look!

When I get back to my room, Gia is already awake and fully dressed. "Where did you go so early?"

I sit down on the Gia's bed and scoot back to the wall. "I had to meet with Dr. Whitacre."

"What for?"

I fill Gia in on Dreya's misdeeds and the subsequent drama that ensued. She just sits on the bed shaking her head in shock.

"Your cousin always causes trouble for you, doesn't she?" Gia asks after hearing the entire story.

I shrug and let out a big sigh. "It seems like she can't help it. As crazy as it sounds, she really thought she was doing me a favor when she bought that paper. I think we're friends again."

"That's not what friends do," Gia says.

Sometimes, someone will say something that immediately makes me want to write song lyrics. Gia just totally did that. I grab my journal off of the desk and start writing.

"You're weird," Gia says.

"Hush! I need quiet."

I scribble furiously. *When you left, you said it wasn't the end/Said you needed a little time/That you had to just make up your mind/When you left, you said we'd always be friends/But you're talkin' 'bout me all over town/Telling your boys I've been messin' around/I'd never do that to you/Wouldn't put you in that position/That's not a friend to me/But tell me what's your definition?/That's not what friends do/That's not what friends do/Lovin and leavin/lyin' and schemin'/Breakin' my heart/When you say that you're leavin'/That's not what friends do/That's not what friends do/If you're supposed to be a friend to me/ Then give me an enemy.*

When I look up from my writer's haze, Gia is staring at me. "Are you back now? Because you totally just went to another planet right then."

"I'm sorry, girl. When the muse strikes I have to listen to it. I think I just wrote my first country/western song."

"For real? What you gonna do with that?"

"Sell it, I hope. Country artists sell a lot of records. Way more than R and B. Evan would probably bust a blood vessel if he heard this song."

"He wouldn't like it?"

"No, that would be from excitement. He would love it, and that's the problem. I don't want him liking my stuff too much. He might start thinking he owns me."

"That's not good."

"Nope. All bad."

I haven't been a part of Evan's "camp" that long, and already I feel myself pulling away from him and protecting myself. Not that I think he's out for anything other than success, or anything, but maybe he's *too* ambitious, and I'm scared for my cousin.

"Gia, can I tell you something that is super top-secret?"

Gia makes a zip-her-lips motion. "You can tell me anything."

"This is take-it-to-the-grave secret."

"Got it!" Gia sounds irritated, but I am dead serious with this.

"Okay . . . so I think Dreya is pregnant."

Gia's mouth opens wide. "Shut the heck up. Why would she want to get pregnant? Y'all are just about to blow up!"

"She overheard that Epsilon Records wants Evan to drop her from the Reign Records label. They are our parent company, and they really make all the decisions."

"So, then she goes to another label! What does that have to do with a baby?"

"I really think that Dreya wants the fame and the money without actually doing any work for it."

"But she's so talented. I mean, getting pregnant by a baller is what groupies and non-factor chicks do."

"I tried to tell her that. I wish she believed in herself as much as we do."

My phone buzzes so I pull it from underneath my bra strap to check the text message.

Gia rolls her eyes at me. "You do know that cell phones have low levels of radiation right? You're going to get cancer of the shoulder or something with your country self."

"Country? Just 'cause you from the Midwest, you don't get to call me country. I am a Southern belle, honey."

"Southern Boo Boo," Gia says while holding her nose.

I crack up laughing at Gia as I open a picture text. Ooh! It's pictures from the photo shoot. Jacinto says, I wanted you to see these first.

The pictures of us all together are really, really cute. I think they'd make a wonderful cover of *Vibe*. The one of me and Dreya screams record sales. When I get to the ones of me and Sam, I drop the phone on the bed.

"What?" Gia asks. Then she doesn't wait for me to answer, she picks up my phone and looks for herself.

"Oh my goodness. These look good. Sam . . . he's so, so intense. He's looking at you like you're the last woman on earth, Sunday."

"No, not the last woman. He brought a girl with him to the photo shoot and let me think she was his new boo, but the hairstylist knew he wasn't telling the truth."

"So, he was trying to make you jealous, because you keep flaunting DeShawn everywhere. You took him to the Grammys for crying out loud. Sam's gotta have some dignity."

I throw one of Gia's pillows at her. "Whose side are you on?"

"I'm not on anybody's side. I just think that you still care about him, even though he's a cheater."

"Not just that! He smokes weed now, too. I don't like that."

Gia throws one hand into the air. "Uh, okay! Illegal drugs are whack."

"Right."

"But you *still* care about him, Sunday. And you need to address those feelings."

I scrunch my nose into a frown. "You know what you need to do?"

"What?"

"Stop giving unsolicited advice."

Gia shrugs and chuckles. "I'm just saying."

I so don't care if Gia is right about my feelings for Sam. I have to admit that the photo shoot had me a little twisted, and having Sam in my personal space trying to make me jealous was a bit much. But she's dead wrong about me needing to deal with anything. The only thing I need to do is let the feelings fade, because that's what feelings do with the passing of time.

There is a light knock on our door. Gia pops up to answer it. It's her cousin Hope and Piper—an unlikely combination. Piper is in tears and her hair is disheveled. Hope has her arm around Piper as she leads her into the room.

"Look who I found wandering around the campus," Hope says as she guides Piper to the bean bag chair.

Gia says, "Piper, you look a mess, girl. You gotta pull yourself together. Linden was a total dog."

Piper looks up and fresh tears roll down her face. "I-I totally get that. Linden was a dog, but Meagan . . ."

"Is as bad as he is, . . ." I say. "She should be mad that he was playing her too, but she's not. I don't understand why you're so sad. Kick them both to the curb."

"Before all of this, Meagan and I were talking about hanging out on spring break and going to Destin together. She even invited me to her parents' house in Martha's Vineyard for the summer. We were going to go bike riding and eat custard out of cups. It sounded wonderful."

Gia, Hope, and I all look at each other. I suppose they don't know what to say either, because I can't think of one word that I can give in reply to this.

Piper continues, "I've never had a friend like Meagan before—you know, someone rich and privileged. It felt like I was going to maybe have the life of one of the popular girls in one of those teen novels Hope likes to read."

I look at Hope and lift an eyebrow. "Don't judge me," Hope says.

"Who in the world cares about popular and privileged?" Gia asks.

Piper says, "That's easy for you to say. You brought your entire clique with you to Atlanta. Hope, your father is a rich pastor, and Sunday is a celebrity! Where do I fit? I was going to pledge Gamma Phi Gamma, but there's no way I'll get in now, with Meagan a shoo-in. She'll ruin my chances."

"Forget about Gamma Phi Gamma," I say. "You, my friend, are a member of the most elite clique on campus."

Piper rolls her eyes and says, "And what's that?"

"My entourage!"

Gia twists her lips to the side. "I thought we just made that up for club night."

"It doesn't have to be just for the club. You are my sisters. And I think I want to take my sisters on a shopping spree."

"How many times she gonna tease us with this?" Gia asks. "Last time you were taking us shopping you ran off to do Evan's bidding."

"Well, this time, I think we should go furniture shopping," I say. "For our new apartment!"

Hope, Gia, and Piper squeal. Then, Hope stops. "Wait. Am I in your entourage? I only hang out with y'all sometimes, but I want to live with you too!"

"Please, Sunday! She can share a room with me," Gia says.

I give a little grin. "Next thing you know you're going to try to move Ricky and Kevin up in there too."

"Kevin *is* your assistant," Piper says. "And he's a hottie. I don't see why not."

Then, I consider the possibilities. Instead of an apartment, I can have a house. A big house that I can purchase with cash, and I can move all of my friends in with me. It will save them money on their college bills, and every weekend will be a party.

"Let's go house shopping, y'all. I think I want a pool."

19

Mystique and I are enjoying lunch at Paschal's in honor of the *Vibe* photo shoot. The magazine's editors decided to use the picture of me and Dreya for the cover, which annoyed Evan, but made Dreya happier than a clam.

"I'm buying a house," I say. "Do you know any real estate agents?"

"Yes, I have a good one. I'll tell her to call you. What are you in the market for?"

"I want a big house. Five bedrooms at least, four, maybe five, baths, a pool, and a theater room."

"Whoa. All that? Where you want to stay?"

"Buckhead, I think. I'm not trying to have to drive too far to go to school."

"Buckhead? Girl, how much you trying to spend?"

"I don't know. Five hundred thousand at the most."

Mystique taps her chin. "You might be able to get something in foreclosure for that price."

"Good. That's what I want."

Mystique picks up the magazine and smiles. "This picture is so cute! It's almost like an alter ego shoot, and who knew Dreya could look that sweet?"

"She is a good actress! And the photo shoot was fun."

Mystique flips through the pages. "Did they interview y'all for the article?"

"Not really. They asked a couple of questions here and there but nothing formal."

"Have you read it yet?"

"No . . ."

Mystique scans the article and breathes a sigh of relief. "You are lucky! There's nothing damaging here. Haven't I schooled you better than that? You always ask what they're going to print before they print it."

"I guess I wasn't thinking about that."

"That's obvious. You also aren't thinking about your figure eating all that fried chicken."

"I know, I know. When I'm old like you, I'll watch my figure. Right now, my metabolism is kicking some serious tail, so I'm gonna eat what I want."

Mystique chuckles. "Okay. You got me. I am approaching thirty. I remember when I could eat whatever I wanted. Trust, you're going to be eating sprigs of lettuce just like me in a few years."

Mystique pulls out her tablet and goes to the Internet. "By now, your *Vibe* photos are all over the Internet. Let's see what BlackCelebrityGossip.com has to say. They'll either love the photos or hate them."

I cover my mouth and giggle at Mystique. Any time she does an interview she says, "I never look at the blogs. I don't care about gossip. Family is the only thing that's important." She checks the blogs religiously, and has a Google alert set up to send her a message every time her name appears online.

"Oh no!" Mystique says.

"What?"

Instead of answering, she spins her tablet around and points. The story says: *Is Reign Records Coming Apart at the Seams? An insider from the* Vibe *photo shoot, tells us that Bethany was high as a kite the entire shoot. Fake lovebirds Sunday and Sam both showed up at the shoot with dates. And y'all didn't hear it from us, but Ms. Squeaky-Clean Sunday just got caught cheating at Spelman. Looks like her cousin's ways are rubbing off on her. Speaking of Drama, she is the only one who seemed genuinely happy as she could barely keep her hands off of her sponsor, Evan Wilborn, but she was also vomiting every few minutes. Was it a hangover, or should we be asking Drama where she's registered the baby?*

"Was Dreya really throwing up all over the place?" Mystique asks.

"She threw up one time. This is such an exaggeration. They always are."

"So she's not pregnant?"

I blink once and pause before responding. "I really don't know."

"You paused too long, Sunday. You know something."

I think I know something, but I haven't talked to Dreya since the photo shoot, so I'm sure not about to confirm or deny anything to her sworn enemy.

"She would choose right now to get pregnant," Mystique hisses. "Just when I was about to make my announcement about my pregnancy."

I guess my silence was all the confirmation Mystique needed. "Maybe she's not pregnant."

"I gotta give it to her, she's smart. Epsilon is dropping her after this next record, so she should have plenty of time to spend Evan's money and raise their child. He sure won't be there."

I narrow my eyes suspiciously. "How do you know about Epsilon dropping her from her record deal?"

"Come on, Sunday. You don't really have to ask that question, do you? She's getting dropped, because I'm walking if they don't drop her. My contract is up after my next record and they want to keep me happy."

I shake my head and move the fried chicken pieces around on my plate. I feel trapped in the middle. Mystique is my mentor. I've been listening to her music since I was in middle school. I look up to her and respect her, but I've got to admit that she's ruthless and cutthroat.

When I don't reply, Mystique continues, "And you're cheating, Sunday? What's up with that?"

"No, I'm not. I was accused, but I didn't do it. Dreya bought a paper for me from the campus hustler."

"So you're not going to say anything about me asking Epsilon to drop Drama?"

I swallow my food and then clear my throat. "I just have one question. Why are you so threatened by her?"

"It's not so much that I'm threatened," Mystique says with a smile. "She has crossed me one too many times. I don't play that."

I'm not convinced she's telling the truth. I think she is scared that someone is going to take her spot. And apparently, she thinks that person is going to be Dreya.

"You *think* she's crossed you. You don't have any proof."

Mystique laughs out loud. "I don't need proof! I just get rid of all enemies in my path. Dreya made herself an enemy to me from day one, so I'm just finishing what she started."

A few tables over, a group of fans wave at Mystique. She turns on her high-wattage smile and waves back with one finger. I guess that was supposed to be a cutesy gesture, but for some reason it irritates the heck out of me. Maybe because she's talking about destroying my cousin's career and pretending to be sweet at the same time.

My phone buzzes. It's a text from my mom. **Emergency family meeting. I don't care what you're doing, get yourself here in an hour.**

I take a hundred-dollar bill out of my purse, and place it in the middle of the table. "I gotta go. It's an emergency. Thanks for lunch, it's on me."

"That's a pretty generous tip, Sunday. Our food is only fifty dollars."

I shrug. "It's cool. We had a good waitress. She didn't ask to take our picture with her cell phone."

I skip the customary embrace that I usually have with Mystique. I don't hug potential enemies, and that's exactly how Mystique is coming across right now. Seriously, how soon is it going to be before she's threatened by me? How long will it take for her to start destroying my career?

20

When I walk through the door at home, my mother is muttering, fussing under her breath. I can make out bits and pieces of what she's saying. For the most part, there's a lot of, "The blood of Jesus" and "I can't believe these heffas" being thrown around. I'm going to assume that I'm one of the heffas.

My mom just looks at me and says, "Sit down. Just sit yourself on down."

I do as I'm told, and glance around to see if there's any evidence of why my mom is talking to herself and God at the same time. Manny comes out of the back room, where he used to sleep, wearing his favorite *Transformers* T-shirt and jeans.

"Hey, Sunday!" he screams as he launches himself into my lap. "You and my sister are in trouble."

Manny always knows the scoop, because he ignores all

rules about children participating in grown-folk conversation.

"I'm grown," I say as I kiss Manny's head full of curls. "What are you doing over here anyway? Do you like your new place?"

"I do like my new house, but there's nobody there to get me water in the middle of the night."

"Why don't you put a glass on your nightstand before you go to sleep?"

Manny looks like he considers this for all of two seconds. "Um . . . then a spider could be swimming in it when I get ready to take a sip. Then, I could swallow a spider and it might have babies in my stomach . . . and then . . . would I be a Spider-Man after that?"

I crack up laughing. "Only if it's a radioactive spider."

"Ooh . . . I got a radio in my room too."

My mother stops her muttering and looks at me. "What are you laughing about? Half of my church has called me about you and this cheating scandal at Spelman. How could you embarrass me like that?"

Manny jumps off my lap. "You might be about to get a whupping."

My declaration of *I'm grown* sounds a little hollow with my mother ranting in my face. Right now, I feel like I'm five years old.

"Mom, I didn't cheat." I stop short of telling my mother about Dreya's involvement. It feels like snitching, much more so than telling Dean Whitacre.

"Then why is that all over the Internet, huh? Don't tell me there's not some truth to that gossip."

"You're just going to have to trust me on this one, Mom. I didn't cheat."

My mother's left eyebrow shoots up so high that it's in danger of leaving her face. "You don't tell me what I have to do! I'm the mother here, and you are the daughter. You done got it all twisted."

"Mom, I'm sorry. I didn't mean it like that. I just meant that I don't have any other way to convince you other than giving my word. I didn't do it."

My mother purses her lips together into a thin, straight line. "I guess I believe you, but you need to explain something else. Why do I have Realtors calling here all day every day all saying that they can get you the best deal on a house? Do you have anything you want to share?"

"Um, I was going to tell you about this. I'm shopping for a house in Buckhead."

"What? Why a house and why Buckhead? I thought you were going to get a condo."

I have already constructed my argument for this moment. I know my mother won't like this at all. So here goes. . . .

"Well, I started looking at condos, and Buckhead is the nicest area closest to school."

"Mmm-hmm . . ."

"And some of the condos are as expensive as a house."

"But you don't need a house! I will be more comfortable with you in a locked building guarded by a doorman. The idea of you in a house by yourself scares me, Sunday."

"Well . . . I won't be by myself. My school friends are

coming with me. Gia, Hope, Piper, Kevin, Ricky, and De-Shawn . . ."

My mother's mouth drops open. "Have you lost your natural mind? You think you're about to have a party house?"

"No, Mom. Not at all. More like a boarding house. They will save money on room and board, and pay me rent. And I'll also have a recording studio in my house, so that I can get my music done."

"Why the boys, Sunday? That's not going to look right!"

"Look right to whom? Your church friends? None of these guys are my boyfriend! Kevin is my assistant and is going to be a minister. Ricky is celibate, and DeShawn is my bodyguard and friend!"

"You think you're grown, don't you?"

I open my mouth to reply, just as Aunt Charlie and Dreya walk into the house. They are wearing matching tracksuits that have their names in rhinestone, looking tacky-phi-tacky. My auntie is now sporting a long red lacefront wig that's pulled into a high ponytail in the front and the rest tumbling down her back like some kind of ghetto Rapunzel. Dreya, for once, has a reasonable hairstyle. It's just her now shoulder-length hair lightly bumped with a flatiron. Her most noticeable accessory is a gigantic ring on her finger.

"Check this out!" Aunt Charlie says thrusting Dreya's hand into my face. "My daughter is getting married to a millionaire. Now y'all ain't gonna be the only ones with cash up in this piece."

My mother shakes her head. "So this is how you're going to deal with the pregnancy?"

"You dang straight!" Aunt Charlie says. "When I found out my baby was pregnant, I went to Evan myself and told him he betta do the right thing. He went and bought a ring the same day, and proposed to Dreya."

"Do you love him?" my mother asks Dreya.

"W-well . . ."

"That ain't got nothing to do with nothing," Aunt Charlie interjects. "He loves her and this baby, and that's all that matters."

"Dreya, honey, you aren't even nineteen. You should make sure this is what you want to do before you do it," my mother says in a calmer voice.

"If she changes her mind, she can always get a divorce," Manny says.

"Be quiet, boy!" Aunt Charlie says. "Go somewhere and play with some toys before I beat your behind."

"I'm just sayin'."

Manny takes off running just in time, because my mother and Aunt Charlie both lunge after him. He screams, "Y'all always trying to beat somebody! I'm calling the people!"

Dreya sits down next to me on the couch. "So, yeah, I'm pregnant," she says.

"Thank you, Captain Obvious."

She chuckles and rubs the palms of her hands down her pants legs. "I'm sorry about the cheating thing. My girl has been doing this for a couple of years and she's never been caught. I thought it was safe."

"But you knew that I wouldn't use the paper, though, so why would you do that?"

"I don't know. I guess I just want you to know that I'm down for you."

I wrinkle my nose into a frown. "I don't cheat, Dreya. If you want me to know that you're down for me, then I need you to keep it real with me."

"What do you mean? I always keep it all the way real."

I shake my head. "No, you don't. You're getting married to Evan? What's up with that?"

"How could I say no?"

"You could've said you weren't ready." Then it hits me like a ton of bricks in a sock. "Evan must know about Mystique. She's pregnant too."

"She *would* get pregnant right now when I am!"

"That's exactly the same thing she said about you."

Aunt Charlie snakes her neck so many times that her ponytail dances back and forth like a long red flame. "What!" she says. "That chick stays trying to steal my baby's shine. But that is okay, 'cause her fifteen minutes of fame is just about up."

"We're not having one of those big ridiculous weddings like Mystique had though," Dreya says. "We're flying all of our friends and family to St. Barts."

"I'm not going," my mother says. "I can't stand by and watch you throw away your youth."

"Yes, you are!" Aunt Charlie says. "You are definitely going to support your niece!"

"What are you going to do, Charlene? Tranquilize me and drag me on the plane?"

Ooh, she called Aunt Charlie by her real name? She must be dead serious.

"If I have to, I will, Shawn. I have supported Sunday and I plan on being there when she walks down the aisle, so I expect you to do the same for Dreya."

"I won't be walking down the aisle, I'll be standing on the beach!" Dreya high-fives her mother.

"That's right! At a five-star private resort that only celebrities use. I knew you'd retire me, baby! The day you were born, I said, this girl is gonna take care of me."

My mother rolls her eyes. "If you insist that I be there to witness this foolishness, I will. I wouldn't want anyone to say that I don't support my family."

Dreya says, "Sunday, who are you bringing for a date, Sam or DeShawn? You and Sam looked like y'all were about to get back together at the photo shoot."

"No, we didn't. That was for the cameras, that's all."

"Yeah, that's what your mouth says, but I know what I saw," Dreya says. "I think I want you to be my maid of honor. I'll ask Evan to make Sam his best man."

"Doesn't he have a best friend?"

"His bodyguard, Leo, and he's not gonna be messing up my wedding pictures with his mean mug. I think Sam would be much better."

"It wouldn't be the first time I was stuck with Sam in a wedding. Mystique would love that you had the same bridal party she had."

Dreya scowls. "Okay, scratch that. I'd rather have Leo or even Big D."

"Since we are gonna be on the islands, I want a red, green, yellow, and black mother-of-the-bride gown! My hair can match," Aunt Charlie says. Unfortunately, there is no punchline.

"Aunt Charlie, do you know those are Jamaican colors?"

"Jamaica, St. Barts, they all the same anyway!"

Dreya says, "Right, Sunday, stop hating on my mom's style. She can wear whatever she wants to my wedding."

My mother slumps down into her favorite armchair. "Lord, what are you trying to teach me?"

"That you ain't in control of nothing!" Aunt Charlie says while giving Dreya yet *another* high five.

For the first time in a long time, I agree with my aunt.

21

My "entourage" is crammed into Gia's and my room, so that we can discuss our new proposed living arrangements. I'm close to making an offer on a mansion in foreclosure. It was appraised at two million dollars, but in this economy, my Realtor told me that if I offered four hundred thousand, I should get it. If not, I'll keep shopping. I'm not in a hurry, and I know exactly how much I want to spend. My mother thinks that I haven't taken many of the lessons she taught me, but I have. One thing she taught me is to never spend *all* of your money. Not unless you want to be broke. No, ma'am, I do not.

"So, how much rent do y'all think you can afford a month?" I ask.

Hope replies, "Well . . . I maybe can handle two hundred a month. I think I can get my dad to do that much."

"Since I'm getting a job," Gia says, "I can probably do that too."

"So, if we each pay two hundred a month, that's like twelve hundred dollars," Kevin says. "What about the utilities? Is the house really big?"

"It's six thousand square feet," I say. "And it is my house, so I will pay the water, sewer, gas, and electric. I think it's fair for you all to pay the cable, phone, Internet, and pool cleaning."

"There's a pool?" DeShawn asks.

"Like I would buy a house in scorching-hot Atlanta without a pool."

DeShawn walks over and hugs me. "You are the best thing that's happened to me since I started school. Will you marry me?"

I laugh out loud. "No!"

"I have something important to say," Kevin announces. "I can only go along with this living arrangement if there are rules."

"What kind of rules?" Piper asks. "If we wanted rules, we could stay on campus."

"No, I agree with Kevin," Gia says. "My mother would never approve if this was just some kind of free-for-all. When I told her about it, she said she wants to visit."

Kevin nods. "I think every bedroom should have a lock, and that everyone should take care to be fully clothed."

Piper bursts into laughter. "Okay . . ."

"I like Kevin's rules," I say. "I want us to all have fun living together, but we should make sure we don't have any uncomfortable situations."

"Right," Ricky says. "Listen, I honestly don't know if

I can do this. I'll try it, but if I can't . . . uh . . . concentrate on my studies, I'm going back on campus."

I say, "Fair enough. It's your choice."

"Didn't you say you were having a recording studio put into the house?" Gia asks. "Is that going to be noisy?"

"Actually, no," I say. "There's a mother-in-law suite in the back of the house. It's totally separate. That's where the studio is going to be. Speaking of that, Piper, I want to hire you to do the appointments and book studio time. I'm going to rent it out to aspiring artists."

"You are such a businesswoman," DeShawn says. "I love that about you."

Everyone bursts into laughter at DeShawn and his declarations of love.

"Do y'all want to take a tour of the house?" I ask.

"Yes!" Gia says. "I've got first dibs on bedrooms—after Sunday of course."

"Well, I have the master bedroom, and y'all can figure out how to distribute the other four. My Realtor is on the way, so the guys can ride with her."

"I am so excited about this!" Piper says. "Meagan is just going to die."

On the way over to the house, Gia has a serious and concerned look on her face. She bites her nails and keeps gazing out of the car window.

"Gia, what's wrong?" I ask.

"Ricky. I don't think he's going to move in with us."

"Why wouldn't he want to move to a mansion?" Piper asks from the backseat.

Gia shakes her head. "He's so different now. It's like I don't even know him anymore."

"You ever thought about going out on a date with someone else?" Hope asks.

Gia spins around in her seat with her jaw totally unhinged. "Hope, seriously! I'm destined to be with Ricky!"

"I'm not saying that you're not, but you're both so miserable right now. He's insisting on staying apart, and you keep smothering the life out of him."

"I'm *smothering* him! Did he say that to you?" Gia is hot and mad now. I think the window just fogged up on her side.

Hope nods. "In so many words."

"Did he tell you to tell me to date someone else?" Gia's voice trembles.

"No, he didn't say that. I don't think he wants to lose you either, but we're in college! We're supposed to be having fun. I've never seen Ricky this . . . well . . . blah!"

"You mean he's not always so dull and boring?" Piper asks. "I thought that was just his personality."

"No! Ricky is one of the coolest guys on the planet. I wish y'all could meet him," Hope says sadly.

"Okay, she's right," Gia says. "The way Ricky is now is a hot mess, but I don't want to date anyone else."

"You don't have to actually date anyone seriously. Just go out and have some fun with someone different," Piper says.

"Like who?"

"Like Rashad," Hope says. "Remember him?"

Gia chuckles. "Yes, of course I do, but he's not in Atlanta, is he?"

"Yes, he is! It was such a coincidence. I met him at a club, and we got to talking. When I told him you were my cousin, he started laughing and talking about how you played him in New York City. He goes to Morehouse."

"Wait! Who is Rashad?" I ask.

"A guy I met at a summer program right before my senior year of high school," Gia says. "He was really cool."

"How about he's the guy that almost stole her from Ricky!"

"Drama!" Piper says. "Y'all haven't kept in touch?"

Gia shakes her head. "No. Once Ricky and I started dating, it felt weird staying friends with him."

"What does he look like?" Piper asks.

"He's fine!" Hope says. "Long locks, very muscular. If he hadn't already hollered at Gia, I so would've wanted his number."

"So, do you want to see him, Gia?" I ask.

She shrugs and gazes out of the window again. "I think that might be opening a can of worms."

"You are pitiful, Gia!" Hope says.

Gia clears her throat. "Okay, so when we move in . . . maybe we can invite Rashad to our housewarming party."

"We're having a housewarming party?" I ask.

"Uh . . . duh!" Piper says. "We are sooooo having a party."

"Thanks for letting me know," I say.

"Anytime, landlady," Piper says.

We crack up laughing as we pull into what's hopefully

going to be our new house. It's huge, though not as big as the other homes on this street.

"Are you kidding me?" Piper says. "*This* is where we're gonna live? I cannot believe this."

Gia says, "Believe it. Sunday is blessed, and God's going to keep opening doors for her because she blesses other people."

This makes me feel a little guilty. I can't say I've been to church all that much since the whole music career thing started and I started school. But Gia is so right. I look at all of this as a blessing.

"Come on, y'all!" I say. "Let's go look at the house."

My Realtor, Vanessa, is already walking up to the door with the guys. Kevin is making a squealing sound, so I'm going to assume that means he likes the house.

DeShawn jogs back to us as we walk up. He says, "Are you sure you won't marry me, Sunday?"

"Boy, stop!" I reply and give him a play punch in the arm.

He sighs. "A love tap."

We walk into the double front doors and into the two-story foyer. The floor is white ceramic tile. That was one of my deal breakers. I didn't want carpet, because I've always wanted to hear my feet clicking through the house. My mom has always insisted on thick carpet, and sometimes you just want to feel the cold floor on your feet.

"So what do you all think?" Vanessa asks.

Kevin says, "It's incredible. I am really at a loss for words, and that doesn't happen often."

"Can we . . . um, look around upstairs?" Ricky asks.

"Yes, feel free," Vanessa says.

Gia smiles as everyone takes off in different directions. "He's going to come and live with us," she whispers. "How could he not?"

I've got to agree that Ricky would be a nut to turn down living in this fabulous house. The master bedroom is downstairs, and the other bedrooms are upstairs. Finally, I get my own space. I haven't had my own room since junior year of high school when Aunt Charlie, Manny and Dreya moved in with us. I'm looking forward to this.

Vanessa walks up to me and says, "The bank accepted your offer, so I think it's pretty safe to say you are now a proud property owner."

"Wow! I can't believe this."

"I have to warn you, though, this is a pretty exclusive, old-money kind of community. It's going to take some time for them to warm up to you. They don't really want a group of rowdy college students for neighbors."

"We're not rowdy, so they shouldn't have a problem."

"Well, your idea of rowdy and their idea of rowdy are probably two different things," Vanessa says. "It will probably be a good idea if you go and introduce yourselves to all of them. Take Kevin with you. He's about as white bread as they come. That boy almost had me accepting Jesus as my personal savior."

I laugh out loud. "But I thought you already go to church."

"I do, but he had me thinking I needed to get saved again."

Piper and Hope come back downstairs into the foyer. "So two of the bedrooms are small and two are large, so we've decided that the boys get two rooms and the girls get two rooms," Piper says.

"Gia and I will share, obviously," Hope says. "But I think the guys want to draw straws or something to see who gets their own room."

"Whatever works," I say. "Come on, I want to show y'all the back patio and pool house."

We go through the sliding glass doors to the back patio. The previous owners probably used this area to entertain a lot, because they had an outdoor kitchen installed and the pool is landscaped to look like a tropical paradise. This is really what sold me on this property, because I could swim all day, every day. I'm probably going to be in a perpetual state of pruniness once we move in.

"It's gorgeous," Piper says to me. "Meagan will want to know why you didn't invite her to move with us."

"No, she won't," I say. "She'll know why."

Piper nods. "She's still dating Linden. She got in very late last night and reeked of his cologne when she came in."

"You should've come to me and Gia's room to spend the night."

"I should've, but I was able to endure it because of this." She makes a sweeping motion to the house. "I don't know how to thank you for this."

"I don't know how many people go around thanking their landlord all the time. I just want you to pay the rent on time," I say in reply.

"I will, Sunday. You won't regret this. We're going to have a blast."

Kevin wanders around the outside kitchen. He yells,

"We are going to have outside Sunday brunches, catered by yours truly!"

Everyone, including Ricky, bursts into laughter. It's good to see that he's joining in on the fun. Because Ricky's level of comfort with this whole thing directly affects the attitude of my best friend. Gia is grinning from ear to ear.

Wait, this is the first time I've thought of Gia as my best friend, but she really is. Even though she's already got a whole pack of besties, I feel closer to her than I've ever felt to anyone.

Piper locks her arm in mine and says, "Sunday, I think you are the first real friend I've ever had in my life. Love you, girl."

"Love you right back." I say.

Why does Piper's tight grip on my arm feel like a friend claim? I like Piper too, but I'm definitely not as close to her as I am to Gia. However, since there's no reason to burst her bubble right now, I'm just going to leave it alone.

There's enough of me to go around.

22

My mother's heels click sharply as she walks through my new house. She's going with me to sign the closing papers today, but this is her first time seeing the space at all. I have purposely kept her from the house, because I don't want to hear her complaints.

"This house is twenty years old. Did you get it inspected?" My mom says after walking through the downstairs rooms.

"I did get an inspection, Mom. Actually, my Realtor suggested that I get two, so I did."

"I don't suppose I can get you to change your mind, huh? You are determined to be a landlady to your ragtag group of friends."

"Why you gotta talk about my friends?" I ask.

My mother ignores my question and ascends the stairs. I know that her issue is not with my friends. She actually happens to like them.

"Where are the boys going to be?"

"They'll be in the rooms down the hall to the right."

She clears her throat. "Do I need to have another sex talk with you?"

This makes me burst into laughter. "No, Mom."

"I don't want y'all getting impregnated at high rates in this house."

"Mom, we are not getting pregnant! More than half of us are virgins."

"Are you in that half?" she says over the staircase.

"None of your business."

My mother stops in her tracks, spins on one heel and starts back down the stairs. "What did you say to me?"

"I was kidding! Yes, Mom. I'm one of the virgins!"

"I don't know what to believe with Dreya walking around with a gut full of human."

"I'm not Dreya, Mom."

The doorbell rings, and I run over to answer it. It's Big D and Sam. They're here to look at the space in my mother-in-law suite that I'm converting to a studio. I want to get started working on that as soon as possible.

"Hey, y'all," I say as I swing the door open.

"Sunday, this place is incredible," Sam says. "Congratulations."

"It is, isn't it?" I say with a smile.

Big D gives me his signature bear hug and spins me around. "Baby girl, I'm so proud of you. You're moving your crew in too, like a baby Zillionaire or something."

"What crew? Your homegirls from campus?"

"Yeah, and the guys too."

"What guys?" Sam asks, his voice taking on a protective tone.

I ignore his tone. "Ricky, Kevin, DeShawn. They're paying me rent."

"Does your mother know about this?" Sam asks.

My mom pokes her head out from one of the bedrooms. "Yes, her mother knows about this. It's her house. I can't tell her who to move in."

"Is he sharing a bedroom with you?" Sam asks.

"Uh! Get some business, Sam! You are not here to interrogate me about my living arrangements. You're here to tell me how to build my recording studio."

I lead a chuckling Big D and a fuming Sam through the back screen doors, past my pool oasis and into the small cottage where I plan on making the rest of my music.

Sam surveys the space by walking back and forth and counting paces on the floor. He knocks on the walls, measures the biggest room, and then gazes down at the hardwood floors.

"It's perfect for a studio," Sam mutters. "But why do you want a recording studio anyway? What's wrong with the lab?"

"Yeah, what's wrong with my spot?" Big D asks. "You about to leave us? Go out on your own?"

"No, not at all, but I want to start producing my own tracks."

Sam folds his arms across his chest and leans on the wall. "You want to be a producer, a songwriter, and a singer. Dang, girl! Can somebody else eat?"

"Yeah, but this is also part of my business plan. I'm going to be selling studio time too."

"Oh, she's a mogul in the making, Big D. Watch out, she's coming for you and Evan," Sam says.

"Can you please put your hateration in check, Sam? Or are you still mad that DeShawn might see me in my underwear?"

"You think I care if you're going to be a sugar mama to some broke model?"

My mouth drops open. "A sugar mama? You are out of line, Sam."

"No. You are! I've done everything possible to get you back, and you won't even hear me out."

"Sam . . ." Big D says.

"No, Big D, let him talk! He thinks he can do whatever he wants with whomever he wants, and that I'll just forgive it all."

"The rumors of my exploits have been greatly exaggerated!"

I shake my head and laugh. "It's not the rumors that broke us up, Sam. It was your lies. How often do you see Rielle, huh? Do you hang out with her every time you're in town? Do you take her on shopping sprees?"

"When are you going to get off of that, Sunday?"

"Never! I'm never going to get off of that. Don't you see? I've moved on. You should too."

Sam pulls . . . no, snatches me into his arms and crushes his lips down on mine. I roughly push him away.

"Does that feel like I've moved on, Sunday? All I think about is you. I don't even go out anymore. All I do is work, because I can't stop thinking about you. I've got a thousand tracks I'll never use, because you're not going to write the songs to them!"

"I see you have a lot of regrets, Sam, but how do I know you won't do this again?"

Sam takes my hand, gently this time. "Stop *thinking* so much! It's not about what you know! It's about what you feel."

"Sorry, Sam. I can't put myself in that situation again. I just can't." I let go of Sam's hand and take several steps backward, widening the gap of space between us.

Big D kisses me on the forehead and says, "Come on, Sam. We need to go. Sunday, you have a beautiful house. I'm proud of you, girl. We'll let ourselves out."

"Sunday, please . . ."

I can't deal with Sam pleading with me. "Sam, let me go! Let us go!"

Sam's eyes look glossy, but no tears fall. His face bears a grim expression as he follows Big D out of my cottage.

Breaking up is hard enough, but when it's like this, it's impossible. Every time I see Sam it's like we break up all over again. The feelings and emotions are the same, and it feels as raw as it did the first time we said good-bye.

I step out of the cottage and call out. "Sam!"

He turns with a hopeful look on his face. This stabs me in the heart. "Yes?"

"Don't come here again. Stay away from me. We can't get over each other if we keep dealing with each other."

"You're not over me yet?" Sam asks, and even still the hope is there.

"I don't know if I'm over you, Sam. It doesn't mean that I want us to get back together, though, because I don't."

I hear these words come out of my mouth, and for

once, I am convinced they are true. I don't want to go back with Sam. Trust is no longer a part of that situation.

"What are we going to do about Drama's record?" Sam asks.

"We're almost done with it anyway."

Sam nods and storms off, with Big D behind him. And why am I crying again, like the very first time Sam hurt me?

Yeah. Breaking up is the hardest thing ever. Especially when only one person wants to walk away.

23

I've got to admit when Evan asked me to meet with him I was a little suspicious. Okay, I was a lot suspicious, but with good reason. I've not really had a good track record with Dreya's men. Her last real boyfriend tried to push up on me and got knocked out by Sam, so when Evan reached out to me for an alone meeting, at dinner no less, it made me wonder.

I'm sitting across the table from Evan at Justin's Restaurant trying to read his mind. He looks on edge, so I've got some nervous anticipation of whatever whammy he's going to drop. The look on his face tells me he's got something on his mind.

"I bet you're wondering why I invited you here."

"Not really," I lie. "I think you heard Dreya's record and you want to congratulate me on another hit."

Evan chuckles. "Sunday, I love your confidence."

"Thanks, Evan, but something tells me you're not here to shower me with compliments."

"I'm here to ask a favor of you."

I knew his true purpose would emerge. "Okay. Out with it."

"Will you do a summer tour with Drama? With her being pregnant, she's going to have to promote her new record well in advance of the release date. We're putting out a single at the beginning of March."

"Dang, that's in a few weeks."

"Exactly."

I groan. I had imagined summer, on the beach in Florida. Hanging with my friends, dancing, partying, and drinking non-alcoholic beverages. Maybe watching a movie or two and pigging out on fried chicken, pizza, and cheese fries. You know, a real break. Touring is hard work, and I've been working enough for ten people. I need some rest!

"There's a rumor going around that Epsilon Records is dropping Dreya from the label, so why would they put money behind her to fund a tour?"

Evan's eyes widen as if he's surprised that I have this information. I expect him to ask me to reveal my source, which I will refuse to do.

"They aren't putting the money up. I am."

This is an interesting turn of events. I didn't expect Evan to have Dreya's back like this. From what she told me it seemed like Evan was almost in on the whole getting-her-dropped-from-Epsilon thing; now he's taking on an out-of-pocket tour.

Evan continues, "I see the confusion on your face, so let me explain. Even though Epsilon is pulling out of Drama's future, I still believe she has what it takes to be a star. If I have to release her independently, I will."

"And the marriage? Is that for real or is that a publicity stunt?"

Evan pauses for a long time before responding. "It's not a stunt. Is she the love of my life? Nah, probably not, but she's carrying my child, and that means something to me."

"And if she sells a lot of records, pictures from the wedding and photos of your royal baby . . . ?"

"It's all good. Money in the bank. If it doesn't work out between us, we can go our separate ways. No harm, no foul."

I don't know about the no harm, no foul part. Who knows how that's going to affect her if they end up divorced? He's making it sound like some kind of business proposition and she's thinking it's a fairy tale. Her knight in shining armor is wearing money green, 'cause that's all he seems to care about.

"Even if I did say yes to a tour, I don't really have anything to promote. I haven't even started working on my next record."

"Well, Bethany would go with you as well. You all could sing the collaborations off your records and do some new material or old. I really don't care. I just want you all billed on the flyers."

"What about Dilly?"

"He's not ready yet. You three are already legitimate stars. If there's anyone that I may drop from the Reign label it's Dilly. I trust that you won't say anything about that."

Ugh! I can't stand when people drop secrets on me without warning. Dilly is my friend, and apparently, I'm still his prom date. Now that I know that his career is in danger, should I suggest he start applying to colleges?

"I won't say anything."

"The tour would be mostly on the East Coast. We're going to do a contest for those who purchase a download of her single at the concerts. They'll be able to win an autographed concert T-shirt and some other stuff that won't cost us anything."

"So this is about driving the sales for Dreya's single."

"For the most part."

"What's in it for me?"

"You'll get paid a percentage of ticket sales. You are the top-billed artist on the tour, so you'll get ten percent of the sales, Dreya will get five percent and Bethany will receive two and a half percent."

A wide grin spreads across my face. "You sure know the way to my heart, don't you?"

"Yep, it's through your pocket."

"I'm a homeowner now, so I could use all the extra money I can get."

Evan smiles. "I heard. Congratulations! I hope that my fiancée and I are invited to the housewarming party."

"You sure are. I'm registered at Macy's, so make sure you bring something nice."

"Sunday . . . can I ask you a question?"

I take a sip of my soda and reply, "Sure, but I won't promise to answer."

"Do you trust me yet?"

That is a question with a very complex answer. If he's asking about music and the industry, I'd have to say that my trust of him is growing, but not yet confirmed. If he's talking about with Dreya's heart, I'm going to have to say a big fat no.

"How about you don't give me a reason not to trust you? Then I think we'll be okay."

"You're one tough cookie, Sunday."

I give him another smile. "I have been called much worse."

Suddenly, Evan narrows his eyes and glares across the restaurant. He makes a quick hand motion to Leo, who's sitting at the next table. The big, brawny dude jumps up and moves across the restaurant so quickly that he reminds me of a mountain lion.

Leo stops in front of a table full of garden-variety groupie chicks. He snatches the cell phone from the one in the middle, presses some buttons, and then hands it back to her.

"Hey, that's my personal property!" the girl screams loud enough for half of the restaurant to hear her.

Leo says something back to her, but he says it quietly, and the girl gets up and follows him to our table. Leo sits back down, relaxed now, but ready to pounce again if the command is given. I need a bodyguard like him.

The girl stands in front of Evan with her legs akimbo and her hands on her very curvy hips. "What do you want with me, Evan?"

"If you had wanted to take a picture of me, all you had to do was ask, Tina."

She sneers at him and then me. "I didn't just want a picture of you. I wanted a picture of you with your . . . let me think . . . side piece."

Evan shakes his head. "Sunday, meet Tina, all-around evil chick and main blogger and photographer for BlackCelebrityGossip.com."

She extends her hand. After a very long pause, I shake it, but it is not a friendly handshake at all. This girl prints lies about me on the regular, so I can't say that I have any love for her.

"Pleased to meet you," Tina says.

"Likewise," I say through clenched teeth.

Tina laughs out loud. "I don't believe you. You need more people."

"I'm not an actress, I'm a singer," I reply.

"You are saucy! You should be a blogger. We'd love to have a celebrity insider correspondent."

"If you published the truth, maybe we could have that conversation."

Tina steps back a couple of times like a boxer being punched. "Ouch, Sunday! Can't we all eat? We tell the gossip we hear, and if our informant doesn't get it all the way accurate, we *always* issue a retraction."

"Girl, bye." For a split second I think about demanding a retraction to that foolish story they wrote about me cheating, but I decide it's not worth it. Everyone on campus knows it's not true and obviously I've not been kicked out of school.

"Evan, you should tell your artists that they should play nice with the Internet bloggers. We can make you, sweetie, and when we don't want to play with you any-more, we can and will break you."

Leo rises from his seat in a menacing manner, but Evan gives him a hand signal and he sits back down.

"That's right, call off your muscle," Tina says. "Espe-cially if you don't want me to report your apparent busi-ness meeting as a romantic tryst with the first cousin of your future bride."

"You wouldn't," Evan hisses.

"I would. I'm not on your payroll, so I eat where I can."

Evan shakes his head. "I called you over here, because I am looking for a blogger to leak some exclusive content for me."

Tina pulls up a chair from another table and sits. "Tell me more."

"I've got some of Drama's tracks that we're not using on the album. They're good, but we just went a different direction."

"What's the catch?" Tina asks.

"It has to be a streaming link, no downloads."

She nods. "Okay. I can do that. Do you mind if we em-bellish a bit on how we came by the tracks?"

"As long as you don't try to make anyone in our camp look bad."

Tina giggles, "I've got a much better idea than that."

"All right then, bet. My assistant will make sure that you get what you need."

"Good doing business with you, Evan. You're the best. Sunday, it was so nice meeting you. I wish it had been on better terms."

I just give her a gangsta-like head nod. I refuse to ac-knowledge this bottom feeder as someone legitimate. In my book, her type is the lowest of low.

Evan gazes across the table at me, with a slight grin on his face. "Tell me Sunday, do you *still* trust me?"

This time I don't reply. This behavior with Tina and her grimy blog is beyond questionable. But maybe this is just the seedy side of the music business that I never see. I think of all the leaked tracks that bloggers magically dis-cover and wonder if it's all a setup.

And if it's all a setup then who is holding all the cards?

24

Since Gia is having company at our dorm (Kevin, Ricky, and Hope), I decide to go to the campus library to get my reading assignment in for my anthropology class. I don't mind her visitors, but Gia is some kind of super-smart mutant who can finish her assignments in minutes when it takes me hours or days to do the same tasks. I need a little bit more quiet time than she does.

When we move into the house next weekend, I'll have all of the space and quiet I need. I hired an interior designer to come in and decorate everyone's room to their specifications. My friends look at it as a gift, and I look at it as protecting my investment. I want every area of the house to look like a model home, which is also the reason I hired a full housekeeping staff.

As I walk across campus, I see Meagan and her Gamma Phi Gamma crew. They're laughing, joking, and all wearing some shade of turquoise except Meagan. She's sporting all royal blue. I guess blue is close enough to the sorority colors without disrespecting their tradition.

I try to rush past without Meagan seeing me, and I'm almost successful, but someone shouts, "I love you, Sunday!" and she jerks her head around. Then, this chick starts waving and walking in my direction as if everything is all cool with us.

I pretend not to see her and speed up, but she is determined and unhindered by a backpack full of books so she catches up.

Out of breath she says, "Sunday! Didn't you see me waving at you?"

"Oh. Hey, Meagan." I hope my lackluster greeting is enough to run her off.

It isn't. She says, "I haven't seen or talked to you in a minute. Heard you guys are moving off campus."

"We are. Next weekend."

"I thought I was supposed to be a part of the off-campus crew, but I guess that's changed, huh?"

Does she even have to ask?

"You'll be moving into the Gamma Phi Gamma house soon enough, right?"

"Yes. Next year."

"So . . . you shouldn't care about us then. You'll have your sorors."

"But I consider you and Gia my sisters too."

I bite my lip, pause and shift my backpack to one arm before responding. "Piper is our friend, Meagan, and you are dead wrong for staying with that guy. How can you still date him anyway after you found out about him and Piper?"

"Because boys play games all the time. That's what they do. College is like an all-you-can-eat buffet for boys. But at some time they'll pick the right girl—the one who was down for them during all of their player days."

"There are too many diseases out here for me to fool with a player," I say. "I don't roll like that."

Meagan chuckles. "You're not giving it up anyway, Sunday, so that shouldn't be a problem."

"Well, if I was, I'd want to know that I wasn't exposing myself. I've got a long and hopefully disease-free life ahead of me."

"Linden will get his act together, and by senior year I'll have an engagement ring. He's here to find a wife, just like I'm here to find a husband."

"At least you know what's important to you. Bye, Meagan. See you around campus."

"So that's it?"

I nod. "Yeah. I'm cool on the whole sorority thing, so . . . you know."

Meagan backs away from me. The expression on her face is stunned, but she doesn't try to convince me anymore. She abruptly turns her back on me and goes back to the Gamma Phi Gamma girls.

I continue on to the library, where my study partner, DeShawn, is waiting in front. Did I forget to mention that DeShawn was my study partner? Maybe because this is more of a study date, and I don't know how I feel about this yet. The date part—not the studying, because I need to do as much of that as possible.

"Hey, DeShawn," I say.

"Hey, slow poke. What took you so long to get here?"

"Ran into Meagan on the way over here."

He frowns. "You mean Benedict Arnold. Why did she hold you up? I can't even believe you were talking to her."

"I don't hate her or anything like that. I mean, she didn't do anything to me, but I don't like how she played my girl."

"Right. She kind of put a dent in the crew."

"She did."

"Good riddance," DeShawn says. "Let's get our date popping. I brought you a present."

I smile up at him (because he's tall, and I have to look up to enjoy his face). "You shouldn't have."

He pulls a candy bar out of his jacket pocket. "This is for you to eat during our study session, because you turn crazy when you're hungry, and there will not be any middle-of-session Busy Bee Café runs. We'll never get any studying done that way."

I take the Three Musketeers (my favorite) candy bar from him and slide it in my purse. The thought of the chocolate and fluffy marshmallow center make my stomach growl, but I'm just going to try to hold off until we've been here for an hour. Then, after I eat my candy, I'll convince him to take me for real food.

"Did you bring me something?" he asks.

"Uh no! No one said that there would be a gift exchange."

DeShawn shakes his head. "I'm going to need you to step your gift game up, Sunday. I've hand delivered food to your dorm, commandeered a limo to take you to a restaurant in the middle of the night, and anticipated your study hunger and brought you a snack."

"Dang. I suck, don't I?"

"Yes, you do, Sunday. Handle your business."

I burst into laughter. DeShawn is a straight-up fool. "But for real though, why do all of your gifts have something to do with food?" I ask.

"Because your two weaknesses are food and money, and I'm broke so . . ."

"My mother says to never say you're broke, but that you're between blessings."

DeShawn gives me a big smile. "I don't think I'm between blessings. I'm here with you, so I'm pretty much right in the middle of a blessing."

I feel myself blush, and I look at the ground. "Come on, boy. Let's get this studying done."

DeShawn places his hand on the small of my back and nudges me up the library steps. I feel a jolt as his hand connects with my body. It's a good jolt, one that doesn't make me pull away.

I think DeShawn missed one of my weaknesses. Food and money definitely can have me twisted, but I'm pretty sure my third weakness is really cute guys who know exactly the right thing to say.

25

_____

"Come on, DeShawn! Can you finish hanging that? It's crooked, and the housewarming party starts in three hours!"

I've been fussing at the boys all morning to put up all of my decorations and paintings. The movers got us into the house on Thursday, and we spent all day Friday unpacking our few belongings. Today is Saturday and it's party day!

DeShawn glares at me from atop his ladder. "Look here, woman. You should've planned this party for next week, so we could've gotten settled in."

"No can do! I want to hurry up and show everyone the house. I'm excited!"

Kevin walks up and stands next to me. "That's a little crooked, DeShawn."

"See!" I say. "I told you, DeShawn. Thank you, Kevin, for confirming what I already said."

"Who's side are you on, Kevin? Bros before . . ."

"You betta watch your mouth!" I say before DeShawn gets to finish his sentence and say something he regrets.

DeShawn adjusts the picture of a palm tree until it's perfect. I love the whole Caribbean motif we've got going here with the decorations. I have a big blue couch in the center of the living room. That reminds me of water. There are tan couch pillows that remind me of seashells. The ceramic tile floors are the color of pearls at the bottom of the ocean. Bamboo and cherrywood accessories fill the house and a giant cherrywood pub table sits in the dining room.

Gia has the entire house smelling like coconuts and Piper has lit sage candles all over to "cleanse" the atmosphere—whatever that means. It's pretty perfect, and exactly the way I envisioned it when I first set foot in the house.

"Can I get down now?" DeShawn asks.

I nod. "Yes, and please put the ladder away."

Gia walks into the room. "The cleaning lady is done upstairs. I gave her a tip and told her she could leave."

"Okay. What about the caterer? Did she get here yet?"

"Yes. She's in the kitchen setting up. Do you need to talk to her?" Gia asks.

"No. I just want everything to be perfect. Mystique is gonna be here, and a lot of Atlanta celebrities."

"Let's not forget about our friends from school," Kevin says. "They're going to be here too."

"Yeah, but they're not that important," DeShawn says. "I hope Keisha Knight Pulliam and LeToya Luckett come. We can ask them out on a double date, Kev."

Kevin shakes his head. "I do not deal with older women. Plus, they have money and we don't."

"They can be our sugar mamas."

I know DeShawn is teasing me with this talk. He asked me yesterday could we start dating officially and I told him that I wasn't ready yet. He was a little bummed until I told him we could keep dating unofficially.

Piper laughs as she walks into the living room. "Nobody wants to be your sugar mama, DeShawn. You need to get some gainful employment so that you can get a woman more than a Happy Meal."

"I am gainfully employed as Sunday's bodyguard and as a model. Don't get it twisted. I gets mine. I've got an underwear ad to shoot on Sunday evening."

"An underwear shoot?" I ask. "Where are the pictures going to be?"

"A few magazines and some billboards in the Atlanta area."

Gia wrinkles her nose into a frown. "So your behind is going to be plastered all over some billboards?"

"No. My front is going to be all over the billboards, including my six-pack abs."

Hope calls down from over the staircase. "I don't believe you have six-pack abs. Let me see."

"Hey! That was a violation, Hope! Don't forget the purity rules!" Kevin says.

Hope rolls her eyes. "Dang, Kevin! I won't forget."

"I'm going to get changed for the party," I say. "Gia, you want to help me pick out something to wear?"

Gia asks, "Do you want me to pick it out or help?

Helping just requires me to stretch out on your bed, nod, and wave at you when the outfit is right."

"You're definitely helping. I know how to pick out my own clothes."

"Sure you do. . . ." Gia says.

The front doorbell rings. The bell is a series of chimes that sound regal yet spooky at the same time. They remind me of something from *The Twilight Zone*.

"Should I open it?" DeShawn asks.

"Sure, but I'm not expecting anyone. Are y'all?"

When no one speaks up, I nod at DeShawn to open the door. He swings the big double door open, and there is a girl our age standing outside.

"Can I help you?" I ask as DeShawn stands next to the door, probably waiting for my signal to slam the door.

"I'm here for you, Sunday. Can I talk to you for a second? My name is Rielle."

Rielle? *Rielle?* First question—why would Sam's side piece show up at my house? Second, who gave her the address? I think I pretty much know the answer to the second question. Sam is the only one who could've told her where I live.

Only because I'm curious about her motives, I say, "Yes, you can talk to me, but we'll do it outside."

"You need me to go with you?" Gia asks.

"Nah, I got this."

"I'll be watching from the window," DeShawn says.

I step outside and pull the door shut. I don't know why I'm so adamant about not having her in my house. It seems like something of an insult to have the trick that destroyed my relationship in my space.

"How can I help you?" I ask.

"Sam asked me to come by."

Instantly, I'm furious. What is he trying to do? Rub in the fact that he still has contact with this chick? I ban him from my house and he sends his girl in his place?

"Why would he do that?" I ask. "I don't have anything to say to either one of you."

"I just wanted to tell you that Sam and I . . ."

See, she's already starting off on the wrong foot. She's trying to have a conversation with me talking 'bout *Sam and I*. All bad. She needs to step.

"I don't want to hear about you and Sam. It's bad enough the lies that he told me."

"Can you please just let me finish? Sam and I were never a couple. I can't say that I didn't want us to be, but I've known him my whole life. We grew up together in church."

"Well, you can have him. Y'all can have a bunch of little kids that sing in the children's choir. Leave me out of it."

Rielle snickers. "Trust me, I'd want nothing more than to have that."

"I know, sweetie." I turn to go inside.

"Wait!" She grabs my arm. "I said that I'd want it, but I'm one hundred percent sure that Sam wouldn't. All he cares about is you."

"Well, he wasn't thinking about me that night at prom, or when he was buying you a computer."

"My prom night was the worst night of my life. He didn't smile for any of the pictures and we hooked up, but it was a horrible experience. He apologized after."

I stare at her blinking and wondering how I'm supposed to respond. I don't know that this changes anything, but apparently, she and Sam both think that it should.

She continues, "He bought that computer out of pure guilt, and the fact that my mother and his mother are friends. I wasn't even involved in the transaction. As a matter of fact, I've only seen Sam a couple of times in passing since prom night."

"That's not what your girl said when she walked up to me at the club tripping out."

Rielle sighs. "Yeah, she hates Sam. All of my friends do. She was just trying to hurt him, and she did a good job of it, because y'all aren't together anymore, right?"

"And you're here now. Why do you care what happens with us?"

She shrugs. "I don't, really, but Sam has always been a good friend even if he doesn't want to be with me right now. He thinks he wants you, and he sounded so sad on the phone. So, I'm doing this for my friend . . . not for your relationship."

"Well, uh . . . thanks, I guess." I have no idea what else to say to this girl.

She turns and walks away, looking about as sad and brokenhearted as I felt when I found out Sam was playing me. She must really care about Sam. That must be a horrible thing to care for someone who doesn't feel the same way.

Now I'm straight-up tripping, though! I wish she and Sam had left well enough alone. Why would Sam want to drop all of this on me now, right when I decided to move on and give DeShawn a chance? Well, I guess the answer to that is kind of obvious. He wants me back.

I remember telling DeShawn that Sam was a one-punch kind of guy—and not much of a fighter. I was wrong. He's scrapping hard for me like a street fighter in a cage match. And those kinds of fights are never, ever fair.

Sam sending Rielle over here was a hit below the belt, and almost enough to bring my new romance to its knees.

DeShawn pokes his head out of the door. "You all right?"

"Yeah, I'm good."

DeShawn steps outside and puts his arm around me. "You don't sound like you're good. Did she say something to hurt you?"

I clear my throat. "No, she didn't hurt me at all."

I'm not hurt, but I'm confused as what. I've shut Sam out based on something that isn't true. What's worse is that I've started something new, and now, more than anything I want to talk to Sam again, but I don't want to hurt DeShawn—especially since he's living in my house.

"Well, you know I've got your back, right? You don't have to keep letting those jealous birds have any face time."

"I don't?"

"Nope, you should only fool with people that hold it down for you."

"And that would be you?"

He laughs. "I'm one of them. But you've got a house

full of people in there that care about you and have your back."

I smile and let DeShawn lead me back into the house. It's almost time for the party, but now I'm not in a party mood.

Gia sees my facial expression and pounces. "Sunday, I forgot I need to tell you something, girl."

She snatches me away from DeShawn and into my bedroom. She closes the door as I sit down on the edge of my bed. I look down at my hands and they're shaking.

"So, what did she want?" Gia asks.

"She wanted to tell me that her friend was lying and that she and Sam are not together."

Gia sits down next to me. "So what are you going to do about it? Are you gonna call Sam, or let it go?"

"What do you think I should do?"

"Is Rielle the only thing keeping you from being with Sam?"

I think about all the things that have happened over the last six months with me and Sam, and truthfully Rielle is only one of many reasons why we can't make things work between us. She was the biggest reason, but definitely not the only.

"No. There's other things too."

"Well, then I say let it ride. If you and Sam are meant to be together it'll happen. That's what I keep telling myself about me and Ricky."

"You're right. I can't worry about it, plus Sam is all the way in New York City, so that's not even gonna work."

"Not with DeShawn pushing up on you in close proximity every day."

"He's not pushing up . . . okay, yes, he is. He really wants to be officially dating, but I'm not ready to go there yet."

"Do it when you're ready. Or don't. We're free-thinking women, remember?"

I laugh out loud when I think back to that speech we got on our first day of being official Spelmanites. We're supposed to change our environment, our situation, and the world by being free-thinking women.

I suppose that leaves me free to think about any boy I choose. And today, I choose DeShawn. Who knows about next week, or the week after, or the week after that! Maybe it'll be Sam again, maybe DeShawn, or it could be someone totally different.

The beautiful thing is that I don't have to decide the rest of my life right now. I can just sit back, relax, and get my shine on. It makes me think of the song I wrote for Dreya!

I'm a star, baby
Nobody checks up on me!

TIME TO SHINE

Nikki Carter

ABOUT THIS GUIDE

The following questions are intended to
enhance your group's reading of
TIME TO SHINE.

Discussion Questions

1. Sunday seems to be caught in the middle of Dreya and Mystique's feud. Do you think Sunday handles this the right way? Should she be totally on Dreya's side because she's family, or should she be grateful to Mystique for helping her career?

2. Sam has made a lot of changes since he moved to New York City. Would you still date him, or was Sunday right to kick him to the curb?

3. What do you think about Gia and Ricky's issue? Is Ricky's breakup reason valid, or is he just not really into Gia?

4. Were you surprised how Meagan reacted about discovering her boyfriend's secret? Do you think Meagan will ever make it back into Sunday's entourage?

5. Should Sunday keep DeShawn in the friend zone, or is he a potential boyfriend?

6. Is Dreya's plan stupid, or does it make sense for her to get what she can get while the getting is good? If you were her cousin, what advice would you give her?

7. What do you think about Sunday's new living arrangement with her crew? Is this a disaster waiting to happen?

8. Do you still feel the same way about Sam after Rielle's visit to Sunday? Does Rielle's revelation change anything?

Read on for a sneak peek of
Nikki Carter's next novel
in the Fab Life series,
GET OVER IT!

Where in the world is my songwriting muse? It's that little light switch that goes on in my brain whenever I get ready to write a hit song. It's my inspiration. My mojo. And for some reason it's playing hide and seek from me when I really need to work on this song for my sophomore album.

I never had a problem finding my muse before. In fact, I never had to look for it. I only had to take out a pen and a notepad and let the words flow. It wasn't work. It was like breathing. Now, I'm sitting on the leather sofa in my parlor with a pen and a pad, and nothing is coming out.

"DeShawn! You need to get these dishes out of the sink right now! You don't have a maid picking up behind you." Gia's afro sways in time with her screams as she stands at the bottom of our enormous spiral staircase.

DeShawn screams back. "We *do* have a maid picking up behind us!"

"Well, she's not here now, so you need to clean up behind yourself! I know your mama taught you better than that!"

DeShawn comes out of the bedroom and leans over the staircase. He's wearing a tank top that shows off his great biceps, and even though he needs a fresh haircut and a shower, he still is incredibly gorgeous.

"Why you gotta put my mama off up in this?" Deshawn fusses.

I throw my notebook across the floor which stops their argument cold. Both Gia and DeShawn stare at me.

"Dang, Sunday, what's wrong with you?" Gia asks.

"I'm trying to work!" I say.

"It's the weekend," DeShawn says. "Why are you working? We're supposed to be going to the Chi Kappa Psi party, right?"

I shake my head. "No party for me. I've got to come up with some songs for my record, and y'all aren't helping with all this yelling."

"Um . . . I'm not trying to be funny, but this house has like a gazillion square feet and you have a master's suite. Why don't you go and find a quiet place?" Gia asks.

"I didn't feel like being cooped up in my bedroom, and the sun is on this side of the house!"

"So you need the sun to write a song?" DeShawn asks. "Are you a plant, now?"

Did I say moving into a house with my six best friends was a good idea? It did start out well. I bought this huge mansion in Buckhead and there was enough room for my besties Gia, Piper, Hope, and the boys. Ricky and Kevin are best friends and they've known Gia and Hope since they were all toddlers. DeShawn is my kind of, almost sorta boyfriend, but not really. We're like an unbreakable clique at this point, so it seemed logical for them to come with me when I moved off campus.

It's been two months and I'm already ready to evict all six of them. Gia and DeShawn fight nonstop about everything from dinner to whether to party or not. And especially chores. Kevin likes blasting his gospel music before anyone wakes up. He gets up at five so that he can "spend time with the Lord." It makes me feel like a heathen to complain, so I don't. Ricky walks around in a constant melancholy state, because he and Gia are in love, but broken up. It's a long story that even I don't understand. Piper and Hope are the gossip girls who talk incessantly. I mean it's nonstop with them. Once Piper fell asleep in the middle of a sentence. Then, she woke up and continued the story the next morning.

I pick up my notebook and pen and leave Gia and DeShawn to their current epic battle and take my non-muse-having self out to the pool deck. Where, of course, Piper is lying out trying to bronze herself in a teeny tiny bikini. Her long hair spreads out on the pool chair like a fan.

"Hey, Sunday," she says. "Sit here! You want a smoothie?"

I start to object, but instead I shrug and sit down on the pool chair next to Piper. "What kind of smoothie?"

"Coconut, pineapple, strawberry, and spinach."

I twist my face into a frown. "So that explains the green tint, huh?"

"Yes, but I promise you can't taste the spinach. It'll give you energy."

"Will it help me write songs? Because I'm not feeling this right now, and I need to record at least one this week. Evan is starting to nag me about the project."

Evan is the head of our record label, Reign Records, and he's pretty stressed out right now because my cousin Dreya's album is about to drop, and he wants to follow it up with mine. He's planning a summer tour with me and Dreya, but I know it's not going to happen. Dreya is almost three months pregnant with Evan's baby, but I'm not sure how many other people in the world know that.

Dreya not being able to tour is going to put more pressure on me to have a hot record. I think that's what's making me so stressed out. Evan stole my muse. He's a muse snatcher.

"I know why you can't write your songs," Piper says after taking a swig of her green goop.

"Okay, since you know everything, tell me what's wrong with me."

"You have lost your balance, because your love life is a hot mess."

I roll my eyes, lie back on the chair, and toss my notebook on the ground. I don't know about my love life being a mess. It's nonexistent.

"You need to call Sam and talk to him," Piper continues. "Once you have closure in that situation, you'll be free and clear to be creative again."

"Who are you anyway? Dr. Phil?"

Piper grins and says, "I consider myself more of a white Iyanla Vanzant."

"Oh my goodness. If you watch one more show on that Oprah channel, I'm going to get the cable turned off!"

"Hater! Kevin and I are trying to improve ourselves. We are on the cusp of greatness."

I narrow my eyes and purse my lips together. "What does cusp mean?"

"I'm not sure, but Iyanla said it last night, so I know it's something I want."

I give her a blank stare and an extra heavy gigantic sigh.

Piper laughs out loud. "You can try to change the subject if you want to, but it doesn't change the fact that you need to call Sam."

I broke up with Sam because I thought he was playing me with a girl named Rielle, but then she showed up at my house saying that it was all a misunderstanding and that even though she really likes Sam, he seldom gave her the time of day. So, basically the reason we broke up is not even a real reason.

But even before I thought that Sam and Rielle were kicking it on the low, Sam and I were still growing apart. He'd started smoking weed in New York City; he dropped out of school and made out with a random chick after somebody dropped some ecstasy in his drink.

Our relationship was already on the rocks and Rielle pushed it over the cliff.

While my heart was broken into a gazillion little pieces,

DeShawn stepped in and got my attention. He took care of me, brought me food, made me laugh, and helped me forget that I was hurting. DeShawn really likes me, and even though I didn't do it on purpose, I started to like him too. So even though I want to talk to Sam, I'm not sure if it would be fair to DeShawn.

It would be easy if I didn't have to see Sam or deal with him. But every time I see him in the studio, the unspoken words hang in the air like rain clouds–heavy and ready to burst.

"I can't call Sam. Too much time has passed, and it would just be weird now."

"Okay. I'm just gonna call you Sunday Tolliver—the one-hit wonder. I hope they let me be in the *Behind the Music* special about you. I will say great things about you though."

"Piper . . ."

"No, seriously. You might never write another song if you don't talk to Sam."

"Oh, shut up. I'll call him."

Piper claps her hands and squeals. "Yay! You're going to get back together, I know it!"

"Wait a minute. I thought you liked DeShawn."

"Well, sure I do. How could I not like DeShawn. He's totally hot and super sweet."

"Do you hear what you're saying?"

Piper nods. "DeShawn is not your true love and he doesn't inspire you. That's all Sam."

"My true love? Who am I, Snow White or somebody?"

"You do look like a Princess Tiana doll."

"I don't like you."

"You love me! Call Sam. You'll thank me later."

Okay, so Piper's logic makes no sense. One true love? My life may be on the fab side, but it definitely isn't a fairy tale. And Sam is more Rumplestiltskin than Prince Charming.

Still, maybe it is time to have a talk with Sam. I have to try and see if it helps with the muse. I'm nobody's one-hit wonder. I've got a long way to go and a lot of money to make.

DeShawn steps out onto the deck, now freshly showered and wearing his swim trunks. I think I'm going to implement a rule where he has to wear a full shirt at all times. I'm just saying.

"Ladies . . ." he says before he takes three quick steps and launches himself into the pool.

"DeShawn sure is fine. . . ." Piper says.

On second thought, is there time for me to pick another muse? I mean, I'm pretty sure I can find inspiration somewhere else. Right?

"Call him!" Piper says as if she's reading my mind.

"Okay!"

I pull out my phone and send Sam a text. You in ATL?

His reply is almost immediate. Yes. Whuddup?

Can we meet? Need 2 talk.

Busy Bee?

No. Not there. I don't want to meet Sam at our favorite spot. Too weird and too many memories.

Where then?

Over Big D's.

I'm already here.

I'll be there in a few.

Today I guess we'll deal with those rain clouds full of unspoken words. Hope Sam has his umbrella, 'cause if he says or does the wrong thing, I'm predicting some pretty stormy weather.